Disney
fairies

TinkerBell

The Junior Novelization

The Junior Novelization

Adapted by Kimberly Morris

Random House 🏠 New York

Queen Clarion stood on the balcony of her royal apartment, which commanded one of the best views of Pixie Hollow. Her eyes seemed to rest on the magical landscape before her, but she was thinking about a place very far away.

The queen was picturing the mainland, where the humans lived, and where spring had yet to appear.

A butterfly, attracted by Queen Clarion's bright blond hair and sparkling blue eyes, settled on her shoulder. He folded his wings, as if he, too, was ready to enjoy the view.

"Have you ever wondered how nature gets its glow?" Queen Clarion said to the butterfly. "Who gives it light and color as the seasons come and go?"

She knew, of course, that the butterfly had not. Why would a butterfly living in an enchanted land ponder such things? In Pixie Hollow it was fall, winter, spring, and summer all year round—and all at the same time. Each season occupied a corner of the magical realm of the fairies. It was only on the mainland that one season followed another, each waiting—sometimes patiently and sometimes not—for its turn.

Right now it was winter on the mainland. Queen Clarion could picture the frosty magnificence of Kensington Gardens in London. She knew how the moonlight peeked through the clouds and glistened on the tiny snowflakes. The butterfly on her shoulder fluttered his wings once, and settled back down.

Queen Clarion's lips curved into a surprised smile. For, you see, she had heard a sound that only she could hear.

Somewhere on the mainland, at that very moment, a baby lying in her crib laughed with delight. Queen Clarion listened as the laugh, invisible but filled with magic, soared out of the crib. It flew toward the nursery's open window, where a lone, fluffy dandelion poked through the soil of a window box. The laugh dove through the dandelion and carried one of the soft, white seed wisps into the air.

A new fairy was on its way to Pixie Hollow. But it had a long road ahead.

The dandelion wisp flew upward. It was carried across the rooftops of London and through the smoke of a chimney. It blew past Big Ben, along the Thames River, and over Tower Bridge.

In Pixie Hollow, Queen Clarion nervously clasped

her hands as she followed the journey of the laugh, still so very far away. So many obstacles. So many things to go wrong.

The laugh collided with the bell of a slow-moving ship. No one on board heard the almost inaudible *ping*. But Queen Clarion heard it, and she feared for the laugh's safety.

But joy is fierce. Joy is strong. And joy is resilient.

The laugh spun woozily as the dandelion wisp swirled, but before long it regained its bearings and continued on. It touched down briefly on the sea, and a jingle echoed across the waves.

Finally, the tiny wisp was taken up by the wind once more, and the laugh was carried through the clouds and blown toward a shining beacon: the Second Star to the Right!

Queen Clarion let out a sigh. All would be well. The laugh was moving quickly now—as eager to reach its destination as the queen was for it to arrive.

2

The laugh approached the mythical island of Never Land with a jingle and a giggle. Faster and faster it flew, skimming the plains, cresting the mountains, and finally emerging over the home of the fairies: Pixie Hollow. The enchanted land shimmered with every color of the rainbow. Wintry woods glistened with snow, while nearby a summery glen was bursting with greenery and vines heavy with fruit. Chuckling happily, the laugh sped down toward the center of Pixie Hollow. There stood a majestic tree, radiating magic.

The soft tinkling sound of the laugh caught the attention of a garden fairy at work. She looked like a flower herself, dressed in a rose-petal tunic. "Look! Look!" she cried, pointing at the dandelion wisp.

Other garden fairies darted from the bushes and flower beds and began to follow the wisp.

The wisp floated over a waterfall, where water fairies played. They all shook the water from their wings and happily ran after the wisp.

The wisp passed under the branches of a pine tree, giggling at the tickle of the pine needles. Animal fairies peeked out from nests and knotholes. They, too, followed.

Light fairies in shimmering outfits dove through sunbeams to join the procession.

Soon all the fairies of Pixie Hollow arrived at the Pixie Dust Tree. They settled on the branches of the huge, magical tree like a flock of chattering birds. Their beautiful wings and clothes glowed in the light of the Pixie Dust Well, which surged in the center of the tree. They eagerly waited for the wisp-of-a-laugh to arrive.

High in the air, Vidia intercepted the wisp before it could overshoot the mark. Vidia—with her purple clothes, raven hair, and superior attitude—wasn't the most popular fairy in Pixie Hollow. But she was the fastest.

She flew over, under, and around the laughing wisp, creating breezes to guide it safely to the Pixie Dust Tree. Finally, the dandelion wisp came to rest on an outcropping of mushrooms that formed a balcony above the well.

The jingle faded away, and every fairy fell silent and waited.

A dust-keeper fairy named Terence approached the wisp, holding a chalice brimming with pixie dust.

He carefully poured the dust over the wisp.

The wisp swayed with a tinkle. Its shining strands shimmered and waved, moved by the magical dust. When it settled into its final form, the wisp was not a wisp anymore—it was a tiny fairy dressed in a flowing white gown!

"Awwww," sighed the fairies. The new arrival was hardly more than a baby's laugh with a mop of blond hair on top.

"Hello," the new fairy said in a shy voice. When she waved, her fingertips jingled like tiny bells and sent puffs of pixie dust into the air. She stared at the others in wonder, but soon she was distracted by the arrival of the Minister of Spring, the Minister of Summer, the Minister of Autumn, and the Minister of Winter. These elegant leaders of the seasons took their places on perches above the Pixie Dust Well, smiling down on the new fairy with welcoming faces. Then they turned to look at a space between the branches where the air was beginning to shine.

The new fairy watched in wide-eyed amazement as a misty cloud of golden dust wove its way through the limbs of the Pixie Dust Tree. Then the mist cleared to reveal a radiant and regal fairy with magnificent wings. It was none other than Queen Clarion.

The queen regarded the new arrival with a warm

smile. "Born of laughter, clothed in cheer, happiness has brought you here," she said. Then she winked at the new fairy. "Welcome to Pixie Hollow. I trust you found your way all right?"

"I . . . I . . . guess so," the new fairy stammered.

Queen Clarion flew behind the new fairy. "Let's see about those wings." With gentle hands, she unfurled two gossamer wings from the little fairy's back.

The gathering of fairies sighed again. "Oooooh!"

The new fairy seemed dazed and uncertain, until Queen Clarion took her hand and led her into the air.

Tentatively, she flapped her wings, rising slowly. She hovered for a moment; then she began to fly with increasing confidence.

The others fairies applauded and laughed when she raced in a giddy circle and turned a somersault.

They liked this new arrival. And each fairy looking on hoped that the new fairy would turn out to be a member of his or her talent guild.

Queen Clarion waved her hand and several dozen toadstools magically sprouted around the edge of the Pixie Dust Well, forming a row of pedestals.

The fairies fell silent. Arriving and flying were all fine and dandy, but watching a new fairy figure out her talent was the most exciting part.

One by one, fairies of every sort flew toward the

pedestals, clutching small objects that represented their talents. Rosetta the garden fairy gently carried a beautiful flower. The water fairy Silvermist stepped forward holding a drop of water as if it were a ball and placed it on top of a pedestal.

Iridessa brought a glowing flower lamp—the symbol of the light fairies.

Fawn, an animal fairy with a long braid, left a tiny egg on a pedestal, but only after giving it a reassuring pat.

Vidia swept past the new fairy with her nose in the air. She didn't give a hoot what the new arrival turned out to be, but she always enjoyed a chance to show off her abilities. She opened her hand to reveal a tiny spinning whirlwind.

More and more fairies brought symbols of their talents. The new fairy watched these ceremonial proceedings in confusion. She looked up at the queen. "What are these things?" she asked.

Queen Clarion led her around the display. "They will help you find your talent, little one," she explained.

"But how will I know which one?"

The queen gave the new fairy a gentle push toward the toadstool pedestals. "You'll know," she said in a soothing voice.

When the new fairy approached the flower,

Rosetta and her friends huddled close together in delighted anticipation. Several of them gave the new arrival an encouraging nod. The little fairy reached for the flower, but the moment her finger touched the delicate bloom, its glow faded.

"Ohhhh." The garden fairies let out a collective sigh of disappointment. But the water fairies were glistening with hope as the new fairy approached the next pedestal. She tried to lift the shimmering droplet of water, but the glimmer around it faded as well. The water fairies sighed.

The new fairy's attention was next drawn to the whirlwind. As soon as she lifted a tentative hand to touch it, the whirlwind faded into thin air. Vidia smirked. She hated competition.

The new fairy was getting discouraged. Now she was afraid to touch anything. She flew up and down the line of pedestals. She passed a seed, a lamp, an acorn, a shoe, an axe, a paintbrush, a large kitchen spoon, and finally, a hammer made from a rock and a piece of wood. As the new fairy soared by, the hammer began to glow.

The fairies murmured and whispered among themselves.

The hammer shone brighter and brighter. It practically vibrated with energy. Finally, it rose into the air. Turning end over end, the hammer flew toward the little fairy. Instinctively, she reached out and caught it. Bursts of light shot out in every direction as soon as her fingers closed around the handle.

The fairies gasped; then they began to laugh and applaud. The new fairy had found her talent! Or maybe it had found her.

3

Silvermist was impressed. "Whoa," she said to her friends Fawn, Iridessa, and Rosetta. "I've never seen one glow that much before—even for Vidia!"

Vidia, who was hovering within earshot, huffed and looked away, pretending that she didn't hear and didn't care. But she did hear, and she did care. Vidia was used to being one of a kind, and she didn't appreciate being upstaged by a little wisp with a hammer.

Rosetta's rosy complexion glowed even pinker. "You know," she said, "I do believe you're right. Li'l daisy-top might be a very rare talent indeed!"

Vidia tossed her dark hair off her shoulder and turned away.

The little blond fairy was still confused. What did it all mean?

Queen Clarion put a hand on the fairy's shoulder. "Come forward, tinker fairies, and welcome the newest member of your talent guild—Tinker Bell!"

Tinker Bell scanned the crowd of gorgeous,

elegant fairies, waiting for one of them to step forward and claim her. But no one did. Instead, they moved aside to make room for a group of gawky, unkempt, tool-belt-wearing tinkers. Among them were a tall and gangly one and a huge and lumpy one.

Tinker Bell's heart sank, and the glow faded from the hammer. It fell from her hand and hit the ground with a dull *thunk!*

She stared at the two fairies in dismay.

The tall, gangly one gave her a polite bow. He wore dewdrop goggles that made his eyes look huge.

His big companion lumbered forward. "Haydee hi, haydee ho, Miss Bell!" he boomed. "I'm Clank!" Something wet hit her in the eye when he spoke, and his voice was so loud it practically knocked her over backward.

The gangly tinker grabbed Clank by the tunic and pulled him back. "Oh, splinters, Clank!" he exclaimed. "Say it, don't spray it!" When he spoke, his words tripped along in a charming accent.

Then he grabbed Tinker Bell's hand and shook it enthusiastically. "Phineas T. Kettletree, Esquire, at your service," he said.

"Oh, foo!" Clank said. "He's Bobble, I'm Clank."

Bobble rolled his eyes at Clank and then turned back to face Tinker Bell. "We're pleased as a pile of perfectly polished pots you're here!"

Tinker Bell couldn't help smiling at their cheery greeting. "Uh, me too!"

"Come on, Miss Bell." Bobble took her hand and they soared into the air. "There's so much to show you." He gestured broadly to the enchanted land below them.

"You have arrived at a most wondrous and glooooorious time," Clank told her happily.

"It's almost time for the changing of the seasons!" Bobble added. "You see, here in Pixie Hollow there are different realms for every time of year. There's one up ahead. . . ."

They flew over a group of pine trees white with snow. A blast of cold air made Tink shiver. "These are the Winter Woods. It's always cold here!" Clank said.

Bobble pointed toward a group of fairies dressed in silver descending from the sky. "Look there! Snowflake and the frost fairies, returning home for—"

"—some well-deserved rest!" Clank chimed in.

"They've just finished bringing winter to the world," Bobble explained.

Next, they flew over a forest filled with red and orange leaves. A fairy hovered in the air, carefully painting the edges of a golden leaf. Clearly this was the Autumn Realm.

"It's the off-season for the autumn fairies, too," Bobble explained.

"But they're always working on that perfect shade of amber," Clank added.

Finally, they approached a lush green meadow, bursting with sunshine, where giggling fairies were chasing a dragonfly. A fragrant mixture of honeysuckle and happiness floated upward, and the three tinkers took a deep breath.

Bobble gestured at the frolicking fairies below. "The fairies of the summer glade still have plenty of time to get ready. Because right now, fairies of every talent are preparing for my favorite season—springtime!"

They turned again, and Bobble pointed to a grassy valley where some fairies were spinning rainbows out of thin air. Others were carefully painting the spots onto patient ladybugs. One fairy was herding a little group of flower bulbs, which trotted along like small children.

"Ohhhh!" Tink blinked, amazed and delighted with everything she saw.

Bobble beckoned to her to follow. "Come on, Miss Bell. You've got to see where we live."

"Welcome to Tinkers' Nook!" Bobble said when they arrived.

"Oh, wow!" Tink exclaimed. This grand, beautiful place was going to be her new home!

But then Clank gently tilted Tink's head down.

She had been mistaken. Tinkers' Nook wasn't in the graceful hills up ahead. It was down in a little dirt-floored valley formed by a tangle of twisting tree roots. It wasn't bright and flowery like the rest of Pixie Hollow. Tinker Bell felt a little disappointed.

"Oh" was all she could say.

Bobble smiled proudly. "Kind of leaves you speechless, eh?" he said, mistaking her dismay for astonishment. Tink didn't correct him. Clank and Bobble flew down into the strange little nook, and Tink tentatively followed them.

But when they landed, she realized Tinkers' Nook had a charm of its own.

Unlike the simple flower homes she had seen elsewhere in Pixie Hollow, the tinker fairies' houses were cleverly constructed of twigs and leaves. And each had its own unique shape and design.

Tinkers' Nook was a busy place, too. Wagons pulled by adorable field mice carried buckets and bushels between the various buildings. Everywhere Tink looked, she saw something new and fascinating. There were tinkers running around in all directions, and the air was filled with the sound of hammering and sawing, happy greetings, and shouts of encouragement.

For the first time since meeting the tinkers, Tink began to feel as if maybe things were going to be okay.

She walked behind Clank and Bobble, marveling at all the different kinds of work the tinkers did.

One group was constructing a carriage using a flower for a canopy and a gourd for the wagon. Another was loading baskets made of iris blooms onto a leaf conveyor belt. "Just taking some supplies down to the workshop," Bobble explained.

"They're taking some supplies down to the workshop!" Clank repeated, just as eager as Bobble to make sure Tink saw everything there was to see.

Overhead, fairies were filling woven-grass baskets with acorns. Bobble adjusted his dewdrop goggles. "Watch out for falling—"

"—maple seeds!" Clank cried before Bobble could get the words out of his mouth.

Bobble pointed to a group of little houses. "Over there is where most of us live. That's your house."

"Hey! There's your house, Tinker Bell!" Clank echoed happily.

Bobble tried to tell Clank to knock it off, but Clank was already flying toward the circular house nestled on top of a root.

"It's mine?" Tink stared at the house. She could hardly believe how cute it was! It looked like a little teapot made out of bark—short, squat, and round, with a curly root on the side that curved like a handle. A jaunty green leaf formed the roof, and Tink caught a glimpse of a chimney peeking out the top.

She followed Clank, holding her breath.

Once inside, Tink gasped with delight.

"We were hoping the new arrival would be one of us," Bobble explained. "So we got the place all ready."

The inside of her little house was wonderful—round and cozy, with wood-grain walls, twig-wicker furniture, and leaf curtains. It was just perfect, as if someone had prepared it especially for her.

Tink opened the closet door and saw a row of green, leafy garments—each one larger than the last.

Uh-oh! The decor was wonderful, but the wardrobe selection was . . . well . . . She didn't know what to say. Clank and Bobble seemed to notice her dismay.

"We rounded up some work clothes—" Bobble began.

"—but we didn't know your size," Clank interrupted.

"Yes, our apologies, but . . ."

"But they might be too big."

"Well, that's only—"

"—'cause you're so tiny!" Clank finished. He stared at her between his fingers, as if he were measuring her.

Bobble elbowed Clank to let him know he was being impolite. "That'll do, Clank."

Tink gave them the biggest smile she could to

show that she wasn't worried. She'd figure something out. There were so many things to be pleased with, she could hardly contain her happiness.

Bobble smiled, clearly relieved that she wasn't upset. "Please come on down to the workshop when you're ready. Fairy Mary will want to meet you!"

Clank and Bobble bowed and left Tink to enjoy her new home. She couldn't wait to see more of Pixie Hollow! But before she could go out and about, she was going to have to put on something besides a dandelion nightgown.

She took a humongous leaf muumuu out of the closet and pulled it over her head. It was the perfect size—for Clank.

After a moment of thought, Tink grabbed a pair of thorn-shears from a table and began to cut. With the help of a pine needle and some spider-silk thread, she solved her wardrobe problem in no time.

Her mop of blond hair fell into her eyes and she pushed it away impatiently. Now, if she could just do something with this hair . . .

She glanced in the mirror and twisted her hair on top of her head with one hand. Her lips curved into a broad smile.

Yep! That was the look.

4

Sometime later, Tink found the workshop by following the sound of hammering. The wide, bustling room was scattered with worktables and carpenters' benches. All the work areas were piled high with woven-grass baskets, acorn buckets, and spider-silk sacks.

On the far side of the workshop, Tink spotted Clank and Bobble fixing a wagon. She hurried to join them.

Using a stone hammer, Clank was trying—and failing—to pound a wheel onto an axle.

Bobble pulled at Clank's tunic. "Stop!" he said. He leaned in to examine the axle. "A five-gauge twig for an axle? Clank, I told you it took a seven!"

"You said five," Clank argued.

"I said seven!" Bobble insisted. "Clank, I tell you, sometimes you can be pretty—" He broke off when he saw Tinker Bell.

Clank stared at Tink. "Who's that, then?" he asked Bobble.

"It's Tinker Bell, you snail brain!" Bobble said.

Clank's mouth fell open. "Ohhhh!"

Tinker Bell couldn't help laughing. She knew she looked different—but she hadn't realized just how different!

Tink looked around. "Wow!" she exclaimed. "Everyone seems so busy!"

"Well, spring won't spring itself!" said Clank.

Bobble nodded. "Indeed, my bellowing buddy—and we tinkers are a big part of it." He turned to Tink. "Allow us to elucidate, Miss Bell!"

"We fiddle and fix!" Bobble began singing.

"We craft and create!" Clank joined in.

"We carve acorn buckets—"

"—to hold flower paint!"

"Weave saddles and satchels—"

"—for birdies, you see!"

"Make baskets and bushels—"

"—to carry the seeds!"

"When preparing for spring—"

"—we do all this and more!"

"Yes," they finished together, *"being a tinker is never a bore!"*

Clank and Bobble ran out of breath and broke off, laughing.

Tinker Bell clapped with delight. "That was great!"

"So you see, Miss Bell," Bobble explained, "we help fairies of every talent with our creations!"

"Unfortunately, all those fairies are out of luck this year," a stern voice interrupted, "unless we can actually deliver these things to them!" Bobble and Clank snapped to attention as a stout tinker fairy flew toward them.

Her hair was pulled back in a businesslike way, and every pocket of her green leaf-tunic bulged with tools. She made a soft landing and did some quick calculations on a birdseed abacus. "The wagon repairs are finished, I trust?"

Clank and Bobble exchanged a worried look—the repairs were far from finished! They stepped in front of the broken wagon to hide the missing wheel. "Uh—yes, Fairy Mary," Clank lied.

"Tip-top shape," Bobble agreed.

"No wheels missing whatsoever!" Clank added unconvincingly.

Fairy Mary looked skeptical. She tried to peek around them. "Then let's see it."

"Um . . . See? Define 'see' . . . ," Bobble said, stammering and playing for time

Clank followed Bobble's lead. "With your eyes, you mean? Uhhh . . ."

Suddenly, Bobble pointed to Tink. "Oh! You have to meet Tinker Bell!" he blurted out, hoping to divert Fairy Mary's attention.

Fairy Mary's head swiveled. "What? Who?"

Clank beamed. "She's new, Fairy Mary!"

"Nice to meet you," Tinker Bell said, feeling shy again.

Fairy Mary's gaze settled on Tinker Bell, and her face lit up. "Ah, rapture!" she exclaimed. "A new charge on whom we can lavish all our tinkering wisdom and expertise! Let me see those hands." Tink held her hands out for inspection. "Crack my kettles! So dainty!" Fairy Mary smiled at Tinker Bell. "Don't worry, dear, we'll build up those tinker muscles in no time."

Tinker Bell giggled.

Fairy Mary turned back to the wagon, all business again. "Now, boys, the deliveries?"

"Aye, we're on it!" Bobble assured her. "Uh . . . as a matter of fact, we're heading out right this second!"

"But we've only got one wheel," Clank reminded him in a not-very-quiet whisper.

"What was that?" Fairy Mary demanded.

Bobble threw Clank a dirty look. "Well, uh, it's nothing, really. Clank was just asking if . . ." He paused, searching for inspiration.

Tinker Bell stepped between Fairy Mary and the boys. "Asking if I can go as well."

Bobble blinked behind his goggles, clearly pleased with Tink's quick thinking. "Good one. Very nice," he muttered to her.

Bobble spoke more loudly now so that Fairy Mary could hear. "Yes. He wondered if Tinker Bell could go with us."

Fairy Mary regarded them all with suspicion. "Oh, very well," she said finally. "Get on with it, then!" she added, just to remind them who was boss. Then she bustled off to attend to the next item of business.

Clank and Bobble jumped into action. Clank picked up the axle, and Tink stood beside him to hide the missing wheel. Bobble gave a loud whistle and a mouse came galloping over to pull the cart.

"Hah!" Bobble shouted, jumping into the wagon as it lurched forward.

Tink turned to see if Fairy Mary was watching their departure, and if she had noticed the missing wheel.

She was.

She had.

And she was laughing.

5

*T*ink rode next to Bobble in the mouse-drawn wagon as they headed to Springtime Square with their many deliveries. Clank trotted along beside them, holding up the axle where the wheel was missing. "Slow down, Cheese! I can't keep up!" he puffed.

"The mouse's name is Cheese?" Tink asked.

Bobble shrugged. "It must be. He always comes when we yell it!"

Tink heard a pitter-patter behind the wagon. When she turned to find out what was making the sound, all she could see was swaying grass and a worried look on Clank's face.

A very worried look!

The pitter-patter grew louder. Tink peered through the weeds and flower stalks to see who—or what—was out there.

She glanced at Clank again. He seemed even more alarmed. His eyes were darting back and forth, searching the landscape and peering into the weeds. Tink's heart began to pound, and she tightened her grip on the edge of her seat. She had a feeling that something bad was about to happen.

Suddenly, Clank lurched forward. "Sprinting Thistles!" he yelled.

Tall, prickly plants came running toward them at full speed. They gouged the sides of the wagon, scratching the paint and poking Clank in the backside.

"AAAUGH!" Clank screamed.

Cheese was so scared that he bolted ahead, pulling the wagon on one wobbly wheel.

The wagon careened wildly down the path with Tink and Bobble holding on for dear life.

As they barreled into Springtime Square, Tink caught a quick glimpse of fairies flitting back and forth, carrying berries, seeds, pots, and baskets. Piles of supplies were neatly stacked everywhere. Then the wagon hit a bump—and soared into the air! Tink and Bobble yelled, and fairies scattered in every direction, jumping and diving to get out of the way.

The wagon landed with a tremendous *THUMP!* Tink and Bobble were thrown to the ground, and Cheese squeaked in dismay.

Fawn ran toward the scene of the crash with some other fairies. She grasped Cheese's bridle and stroked his nose. "Easy . . . Easy . . . ," she said in a soothing voice. The frightened mouse immediately began to calm down. "Easy, boy," she continued. "It's all right. Fawn's got you."

Tink sat up, woozy and disoriented. Silvermist ran toward her. "Easy," Silvermist said, imitating Fawn's tone. "Easy, girl. It's all right. Silvermist's got you." She earnestly stroked Tink's nose—which really didn't do much more than tickle.

Rosetta and Iridessa flew to join them. "Ooooh! Are you all right, sugarcane?" asked Rosetta.

Tink tried to sit up, but Iridessa pushed her back down. "Be careful, Rosetta, she may faint!" Iridessa cried anxiously. "Elevate her legs! No, wait!" She pulled Tink back up. "I mean, I mean, her head! Wait, wait, wait. . . ." Iridessa chewed on a nail, muttering to herself. She was obviously trying to remember what they had told her in fairy-aid training. Then she snapped her fingers.

"If she's red, raise the head; if she's pale, raise the tail!" Iridessa cried triumphantly. She grabbed Tink's face and smooshed her cheeks between her hands. "Does she look pale or red?" she asked her friends.

There was an awkward silence as the other fairies examined Tink.

"She looks squished," Rosetta finally answered.

Iridessa's glow flickered with embarrassment as she realized she had gone a little overboard with the fairy aid. "Sorry," she said to Tink, letting go of her face. Tink did her best to smile reassuringly at the light fairy.

"Here, let me, raindrop," Silvermist said. She took Tink's arm and helped her up. "What happened to you, anyway?" she asked.

"Well, I . . ." Tinker Bell didn't even know where to begin. Just then, Clank and Bobble popped up from beneath a pile of berries. "Sprinting Thistles!" Clank declared in answer to Silvermist's question.

Fawn, Rosetta, Silvermist, and Iridessa all gasped.

Rosetta angrily put her hands on her hips. "Those weeds are an absolute menace! Always trampling things, poking people in the petunia. . . ."

Iridessa nodded in agreement. "I always say to steer clear of Needlepoint Meadow!"

Tinker Bell looked around and gasped in dismay when she saw that the tinkers' wagon had crushed a whole patch of blossoms. "Oh, no! Your flowers!"

Rosetta quickly waved away Tink's concern. "Don't get your wings in a bunch," she said, laughing. "It's nothing a little stem-tuck and a petal-lift can't cure!"

Tink felt a rush of pride as she watched Bobble and Clank straighten the wagon and organize the pots and gardening supplies in the back. The garden fairies couldn't do what they did without the help of the tinker fairies.

"Gather round, ladies," Bobble invited. "We've brought some selections from the new spring line of tinker specialties!"

"What did you bring?" Iridessa's glow flickered with anticipation.

"Show us!" Silvermist urged.

Bobble handed Iridessa several tubes made of bark. "Your rainbow tubes, Iridessa."

Iridessa snatched the tubes gratefully. "Finally! Silvermist, could you help me?"

Silvermist smiled and sprayed a fine mist of water into the air. Iridessa flew through it, spreading her arms and creating a rainbow with her pixie dust. Then she landed, grabbed an edge of the rainbow, and rolled it into a tube.

Tinker Bell was astounded. "What are you going to do with that?" she asked.

"I'm going to take it to the mainland!"

"What's the mainland?" asked Tink.

"It's where we're going to change winter into spring!" explained Silvermist. "The seasons change all the time there."

"I'll get to apply my artistic sensibilities," Rosetta said with a smile. She accepted a pussy willow paintbrush from Clank, dipped it in a nearby bucket, and began painting a blossom.

Fawn took a milkweed-pod satchel from Bobble's hands and dropped a handful of nuts into it. "And I'll have breakfast ready for all the little fuzzies coming out of hibernation!"

Tink was just about to ask how to get to the mainland when Iridessa took her hand and pulled her into the air. Iridessa pointed toward the sky. "We just follow the Second Star. . . ."

"Then we ride the breeze and follow the waves . . . ," Silvermist added.

"All the way across the sea . . . ," Rosetta said, taking up the story.

"And there it is." Fawn smiled, waving her hand to create a sparkling cloud of pixie dust.

The whole thing sounded so exciting and so beautiful, it took Tink's breath away. She struggled for words. "Wow—the mainland sounds . . . sounds . . ." She couldn't think of a word powerful enough, so she made one up. ". . . flitterific!"

Tink's new friends looked at each other and shrugged modestly.

"Ah, yes, the glamourous lives of the nature fairies," Bobble teased. "We'd love to stay and chat . . ."

". . . but we tinkers have *real* work to do," said Clank with a smile and a wink.

"Oh, hush, you!" Rosetta laughed, rolling her eyes.

Bobble and Clank motioned to Tink to follow, and the three tinkers darted back to the wagon as the fairies teased them. Tink could tell that this good-natured back-and-forth was as much a part of the routine as the deliveries were.

She took her seat on the wagon next to Bobble. Clank picked up the axle. Tink turned and waved at her new friends. "Nice to meet you all."

"You too!" cried Fawn.

"Fly with you later," promised Silvermist.

6

*B*obble pulled Cheese to a stop as the wagon rolled into Flower Meadow. Bobble consulted his leaf-scroll list. "Here we are. Pretty large order of pollen pots for the—hey!" He flinched as a purple blur zipped past them with a *whoosh!*

The blur slowed for a moment. It was Vidia. She twirled around and around, whipping the air into a funnel of wind. The funnel hovered over a flower, sucking up the pollen. Then it moved to another flower and repeated the trick.

Tink was mesmerized as she watched the pollen-yellow whirlwind gather more and more dust out of the flowers. Neither Clank nor Bobble seemed to pay much attention. She guessed they had seen all this before. But Tink was fascinated, and she wanted to learn more about this fairy.

Clank unloaded some pollen pots, and Bobble looked at his leaf scroll, figuring out their next stop. "The last thing is berry bushels to deliver to the glen—"

"Is it okay if I catch up with you later?" Tink interrupted.

Bobble shrugged. "I suppose."

"Can you find your way back?" Clank asked. He put down the last of the pots and took up the axle again.

Tinker Bell's eyes were still glued on Vidia. "Yeah, yeah," she agreed absently. "Sure I can."

"All right, then," Bobble said.

"Just be careful," Clank added, breaking into a trot.

As the wagon rumbled off, Tinker Bell flew over the flowers and followed behind Vidia, who was busy guiding the whirlwind toward the pollen pots. "Hi there!" Tink exclaimed.

Her voice startled Vidia so much that she lost control of the pollen-filled whirlwind. The stray wind spun away from the two fairies, throwing pollen everywhere and knocking over the carefully stacked pots.

"Sorry," Tink said, wincing. Vidia glared at her; pollen was swirling in the air between them. This wasn't going at all the way Tink had hoped. She smiled sheepishly and tried again. "Vidia, right?"

"*Ah-CHOO!*" Vidia sneezed violently, and her black ponytail momentarily flipped forward. Then, without a word, she flew away to continue her work.

But Tink was determined to make friends. "We

didn't officially meet," she said. "I'm Tinker Bell."

Vidia came to a stop and gave her a long look. "Oh, yes. The new girl."

"That's right," Tink responded happily. "So what's your talent?" she asked.

Vidia began spinning again, until she was nothing but a blur. When she slowed down enough to be visible, she fixed Tink with a cocky glare. "What do you think it is?" she challenged.

Tink bit her lip. "Um . . . you're a pollen . . . *izer*?"

Vidia skidded to a stop, outraged.

"Pollen*ator*?" Tink tried again.

Vidia's eyes narrowed.

"Pollen picker? Pollen plucker!" Tink was starting to feel anxious. She was clearly getting on Vidia's nerves.

Vidia looked at Tinker Bell. "I am a fast-flying fairy," she proudly announced. "A true, rare talent. And this is but a small part of what I do. I make breezes in the summer, blow down leaves in the fall . . . and my winds even brought you here, dear. Fairies of every talent depend on me."

Tinker Bell smiled. "Hey!" she said. "That's just like what I do!"

Vidia snorted. "Excuse me?"

"I mean, tinkers help fairies of every talent, too! So we're kind of the same, you know?"

Vidia's wings fanned slowly. She draped an arm over Tink's shoulders and leaned close. "Sweetie, *I* make forces of nature. *You* make pots and kettles. I work up in the sky and you work down in a ditch."

"Hey—" Tink started, ready to correct Vidia.

"Oh, don't get me wrong, sunshine," Vidia interrupted. "Being a tinker is really swell and all. But I wouldn't go around bragging about your talent. It's not like spring depends on you."

Tinker Bell refused to be put down. "Of course it does!" she exclaimed. "And when I go to the mainland, I'll prove just how important we are!"

Vidia looked confused. "When *who* goes to the mainland?" she asked.

Tink almost rolled her eyes. "Me, of course! For spring?"

Vidia smiled. It wasn't a very nice smile. "Oh . . . oh, of course!" she said. "You'll *prove* it, huh?"

"Yes, I will!" Tink said fiercely.

Vidia's nasty smile got bigger. "Well, I, for one, will be looking forward to that," she said. "Excuse me." She flew off so fast, Tink could hardly see her go.

"No," Tinker Bell called after her, "excuse *me*."

Okay. So it wasn't much of a comeback—but at least Tink had the last word.

7

Tinker Bell flew over Pixie Hollow, replaying in her mind the exchange with Vidia. "Mine is a rare talent," she muttered out loud, mimicking Vidia's sarcastic voice.

Tink snorted in disgust. "Ugh! I'll show her what a rare talent is when I . . ." She broke off as a glint of light caught her eye. It was coming through the trees below.

Curious, Tink flew down to investigate. She followed the glint to a sandy cove near where the ocean's waves lapped gently against Never Land's shore. She landed where she thought she'd seen the glint and began digging with her hands.

Before long, Tinker Bell uncovered a silver coin. She turned the coin from side to side, watching it catch and reflect the fading rays of the sun. It sparkled so beautifully!

Are there any more of these? she wondered. She began to dig again.

The sand yielded treasure after treasure.

First she unearthed a huge brass screw. She spun it on her finger.

Then Tink found a spring. She loved the way she could push and pull it and then watch it snap back into shape with a defiant *sproing!*

But the most fascinating thing she found was an eyeglass lens about the size of a fairy's window. Tink put her hand behind it and watched the lens magnify and distort her fingers. She laughed out loud.

Tinker Bell hurried to gather up all her treasures, piling them into a wobbly stack in her arms.

Tink smiled happily. She wasn't just a tinker fairy—she was a treasure-finding fairy! Here she was, brand-new to Pixie Hollow, and already she had discovered these amazing things. Tink wasn't sure just how, but she knew that with these treasures, she would surely find a way to prove herself.

Then Vidia would see how important a tinker fairy could be!

8

"*H*ey, Tink, what have you got there?" Bobble looked up from his bench when Tink flew into the workshop with her armful of treasures.

"I don't know. I just found them." She plopped the treasures down on her worktable. Clank and Bobble hurried to examine them.

"Lost Things," Clank said.

Tinker Bell frowned. "Lost Things?"

Bobble nodded. "Aye. Stuff gets lost and washes up on Never Land from time to time. You know— from the mainland."

"These come from the mainland?" Tink asked. That place sounded more fascinating all the time!

But she was disappointed when Bobble added, "Not much good for anything, though, eh, Clank?"

Before Clank could answer, Fairy Mary came bustling by with her seed abacus and checklist, busily taking note of the items and supplies. "Berry bushels. Check. Pollen pots. Check." She absently glanced at

Tink's worktable. "Lost Things. Check—" Fairy Mary broke off with a frown. "Lost Things? Why are you fiddling with that junk?"

Tinker Bell shrank under Fairy Mary's disapproving glare. "Oh . . . um . . . ," she stuttered. "They were just so unusual. . . ."

"Mustn't be wasting your time with that rubbish," Fairy Mary scolded. "And I won't have it cluttering up my workshop." She shot a stern look at Clank and Bobble. "And as for you two—no more dillydallying around. Don't forget about the Queen's Review tonight. Goodness! There's still so much to be done."

Fairy Mary started to gather up the Lost Things and flew away with her arms full.

Clank noticed Tink's disappointed look. "Sorry about your trinkets, Miss Bell."

"We'd best be getting ready for the review anyway," Bobble reminded her.

Tink lifted her head. "What is the Queen's Review?"

Bobble rubbed his hands in anticipation. "The queen is going to review all the preparations for spring."

Clank smiled. "It's a good time for us tinkers to show what we can do, eh?"

"Indeed!" Bobble confirmed.

"Really?" Tink's spirits brightened considerably.

Clank jerked his head toward the wagon. "Like me. I can be a wheel," he joked as he and Bobble headed back to their worktables.

Tink didn't laugh. Her mind was already racing ahead, making plans. *Perfect . . . that's my chance!* she thought.

Tink dove into action. She gathered twigs, sap, walnut shells—even silk from a surprised but good-natured spider.

Her moment was coming, and she had to be ready.

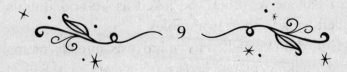
That night, Springtime Square was full of fairies feverishly working to make everything ready for the Queen's Review.

Flower-painting fairies lined up buckets of fresh-squeezed flower paint. Planting fairies stacked bushels of seeds and nuts to be counted.

Ladybugs stood in rows. Some waited patiently for their black dots to be applied; others still needed their first coat of red. A fairy waved them over. "Okay, everybody, turn!" she called to the line of bugs. "Ready for the base coat over here!"

Fawn, Rosetta, Iridessa, and Silvermist were busy with their own tasks, and Clank and Bobble hurried from group to group, lending a hand wherever they were needed.

The Minister of Spring floated through the square, overseeing everything. His face was serious, but his clothes were joyous and colorful. He wore a long, blue robe, with a pink azalea blossom on his lapel.

A garland of leaves held the minister's long hair off his high forehead as he bent over his leaf-scroll checklist. "Splendid, splendid," he said.

He noticed a group of fairies who were unloading berry pots in a hurry—and making a mess in the process. "Stack those neatly! Plenty of time before the queen arrives—"

He broke off when he heard a tinkling sound. "Oh! She's here? Play, music fairies, play!" he instructed.

A band of music fairies struck up a tune, signaling the others to line up along the pathway. The fairies hurried to take their places.

Queen Clarion came gliding in with the Minister of Fall, the Minister of Winter, and the Minister of Summer behind her.

The Minister of Spring bowed with great dignity. "Queen Clarion! Queen Clarion, Your Illustriousness! As the Minister of Spring, I welcome you to Springtime Square!"

"What, no fireworks, Minister?" Queen Clarion teased gently.

The Minister of Spring looked panicked. "Oh— well, I— That could be arranged." He glanced around desperately. "Light fairies! *Light fairies!*"

Queen Clarion giggled. "I'm teasing. You always make such a fuss, and everything always turns out wonderfully."

The Minister of Spring relaxed and laughed. "Well, I think you'll find we have things well in hand." He pointed at a large, closed flower growing on an ornate platform. "When the Everblossom blooms, we will be ready to bring spring to the mainland!"

"Music to my ears!" Queen Clarion turned to the crowd. "I know you've all put in months of practice and preparation. But keep up the good work these last few days. Because just as fairies—"

The queen broke off in surprise when Tink came hurtling along in her wagon. Tink pulled Cheese to a screeching halt, jumped out, and shouldered her way through the crowd to the front.

"Queen Clarion!" Tink shouted. "Did I miss anything?" The music squawked to a halt, and the crowd turned toward Tink, annoyed and surprised.

"No, no, no!" the Minister of Spring exclaimed.

"Whew!" Tink pretended to wipe her brow in relief and grinned. "Good!"

The Minister of Spring stepped forward to send Tink away, but Queen Clarion put a hand on his shoulder. "It's all right," she told him.

Tink motioned for the fairies in front of the wagon to make room. She lifted the leaf tarp that covered the back. "I came up with some fantastic things for tinkers to use when we go to the mainland. Let me show you."

The queen's eyebrows rose in surprise.

Some of the fairies in the crowd whispered. Others glared.

"Tinkers on the mainland? What is she talking about?" Iridessa asked.

"Didn't anyone tell her?" Silvermist added.

Tink heard the whispering, but she did her best to ignore it. She knew that once they got a look at her inventions and understood how important they were, nobody would ever whisper or glare at her again.

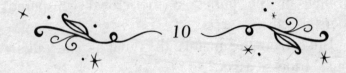

*T*ink held up her first invention. The contraption looked like a nutcracker made of sticks, rocks, and grass twine.

She turned to Fawn.

"Baby chipmunks can't eat the whole nut, right? Their little teeth can't chew big bites." Tink placed a big nut in the contraption and began to crank. "You just turn this—and . . ."

The rocks pressed on the shell from either side, tighter and tighter. But instead of cracking—

BLAM!

The nut shot out of the device and smacked a baby squirrel right in the nose.

The little creature stood stock-still, shocked. Then his big, dark eyes welled up with tears and his furry little chin quivered. There was a terrible silence in Springtime Square, until the squirrel let out a wail and ran off. All the fairies watched, horrified.

Tink did her best to smile. "Whoops. Just have to adjust the gears a little . . ."

Queen Clarion held up her hand, trying to stop her. "Tinker Bell—"

But it was no use. Tink kept right on. She knew she could do this. Her next invention was sure to go over better.

"I made this, too." She pulled out a spray gun made from an acorn, with several reed-nozzles. "It's a berry-paint sprayer! Allow me to demonstrate."

Tinker Bell turned the wooden handle and . . . *KERBOOM!*

The contraption exploded, covering the Minister of Spring with berry paint.

"Sorry! Kind of a work in progress," Tinker Bell explained. This wasn't going so well. She felt a hand on her shoulder and looked up at the queen.

Queen Clarion's eyes were understanding and full of sympathy, but her voice was firm. "Tinker Bell, sweetheart, has no one explained?"

Tinker Bell bit her lip. Her heart pounded and she felt her throat tighten. She had a bad feeling that whatever Queen Clarion was going to say wasn't something she wanted to hear. "Explained what?" she asked quietly.

"Tinker fairies don't go to the mainland, dear."

"What?" Tink whispered.

"All of those things are done by the nature fairies. Your work is here, in Pixie Hollow."

"But . . . but . . . I thought . . ." Tinker Bell's voice trailed off.

"I'm sorry, Tinker Bell," the queen said softly.

Tink looked at the assembled fairies. Some would not meet her eyes. Others gazed at her sympathetically.

Only Vidia seemed to be enjoying Tink's heartbreak. Her face was twisted in a mean smirk. Tink didn't want to give her any satisfaction. She tried to pull herself together.

"Oh . . . okay. That's . . . um . . . good! I mean, I really couldn't make it anyway, so this actually works out . . . good!" She took the reins and began leading Cheese away, trying not to look at the crowd as it parted for her.

"Music fairies!" the Minister of Spring called out. The music fairies burst into feverish song, desperate to fill the unhappy silence.

Iridessa and Fawn hurried toward the wagon, with Clank and Bobble running behind them. Rosetta and Iridessa flew along, too.

But Tink turned away from them. She shook the reins to hurry Cheese, eager to disappear into the dark so that she could cry undisturbed.

11

Back in the empty workshop, Tink dropped her contraptions on her worktable and slumped down on her stool.

"Back so soon?" said a voice.

Tink spun around in surprise.

Fairy Mary stood on the far side of the workshop, checking on supplies and making tick marks in her leaf notebook.

"You didn't go?" Tinker Bell asked.

"Oh, goodness, no. Far too much work to do down here."

Tink watched Fairy Mary cheerfully counting pots and wondered how she could be so satisfied. "Vidia was right. Being a tinker stinks," she muttered.

"Excuse me? What was that?" Fairy Mary looked up from her checklist.

"Why don't *we* get to go to the mainland?" Tinker Bell blurted.

Fairy Mary snickered. "The mainland? Who gives

a pile of pebbles about the mainland?"

"But, Fairy Mary, the other fairies get to go."

Fairy Mary put her hands on her hips. "Now, Tinker Bell, are you a garden fairy?"

Tinker Bell knitted her brows. "Well, no."

"Are you a light fairy?"

"No."

"Animal fairy? Water fairy, perhaps?"

"No and no."

Fairy Mary shook her head. "No. You're not. You are a *tinker*. It's who you are. Be proud of it." She began to fly away, pausing to add, "The day you can magically make the flowers grow, or capture the rays of the sun or whatnot, then you can go. Until then, your work is here." With that, she was gone.

Tink let her head fall on the table in despair. There had to be something better in store for her than this—a pile of failed inventions and no trip to the mainland. There just had to be.

Thanks to Fairy Mary's words, it wasn't long before she had a brand-new idea.

Tink spread her wings and zipped into the air.

She had a foolproof plan, and when the Everblossom bloomed, she would be among the fairies leaving for the mainland. This time for sure!

12

The next morning, Tink arrived early at the Pixie Dust Well. All the fairies began their day by lining up for their daily dose of dust. They were chatting while they waited. Tinker Bell ducked out of sight and waited to make an entrance.

"Great festival yesterday!" a flower fairy called out to her friend.

"Nice day for flying!" another fairy said.

Tink saw Iridessa, Fawn, Rosetta, and Silvermist, who were waiting to receive their dust from Terence. "Here you go, Silvermist," he said.

Silvermist closed her eyes and held her nose when Terence poured the dust on her. "Thank you, Terence," she said in a nasal voice. Then she turned back to her friends. "I hope Tinker Bell is okay," she said.

Terence started to pour dust on Rosetta, but she politely stopped him and produced her own flower powder-puff. She delicately dipped it into the dust and gave herself a quick powder. "That poor little sapling. She looked pretty wilted yesterday."

"I wouldn't blame her if she stayed in bed all day!" Iridessa agreed, stepping up for her dust.

Tink listened from her hiding spot and smiled. Her friends were going to be so amazed when she told them about her great new plan!

The four fairies were indeed startled when Tinker Bell popped out. "Hey, Iridessa! Morning, girls!"

Terence was so surprised by Tink's perky manner that he dropped his dust ladle on Iridessa's head with a *bonk!*

Tink gave them a big smile.

"Tinker Bell!" Fawn cried in happy surprise.

Tink did a fancy spin around a branch and then proudly landed on it. "Guess what?" she announced. "I've decided I'm not going to be a tinker fairy anymore!"

Fawn and Iridessa looked shocked.

Rosetta and Silvermist looked bewildered.

And all four spoke at once. "What?"

"Well," Tink said, "I was thinking, why do I have to be a tinker? Just because some silly hammer glowed? Who's to say it wasn't a mistake? Maybe I can just switch my talent!"

"Switch your talent?" Rosetta echoed in a faint voice. "I don't know, Tinker Bell."

"If you could teach me your talents, maybe I could

show the queen that I can work with nature, too." A gnat landed on Tink's arm as she spoke, and she absentmindedly slapped at it. Fawn's eyebrows shot up in dismay. "Then she'd let me go to the mainland for spring!" Tink finished.

"Oh, Tinker Bell. That's just not how it works," Rosetta told her sadly.

"Well, maybe she could," Fawn said, sounding intrigued with the idea.

Silvermist was downright enthusiastic. "She's right! She could!"

Iridessa wasn't buying it. Even her glow looked unsure. "Well, I've never heard of someone switching talents before."

Silvermist reconsidered. "She's right! Me neither!"

"Look," Tink pleaded. "You all do things that are beautiful, and magical, and important. But me . . ." Tink could tell she was starting to sound desperate. But, well, she *was* desperate! "There's got to be more to my life than just pots and kettles. All I'm asking is that you give me a chance."

The group exchanged uneasy glances.

Finally, Silvermist stepped forward and took Tink's hand. "I'll help you, Tinker Bell."

Tink's heart soared. "Oh, thank you, Sil!"

"Me too," Fawn said. "Could be fun!"

Rosetta shrugged. "Well, there's a first time for

everything, I guess. What harm can come from trying?"

Iridessa was the last holdout. But Tinker Bell made her eyes so big and her smile so hopeful that Iridessa finally caved. "Okay. But I refuse to be held responsible for any calamities or catastrophes that result from this."

13

*T*heir first stop was Lilypad Pond, where a gentle stream ran through the grass-lined pool.

Silvermist and Tink flew over the area, with Fawn, Rosetta, and Iridessa right behind them.

Silvermist was trying to decide where to start. "For your first day of water-fairy training, I could show you how to make ripples in the pond . . ."

Tink nodded. "Okay!"

"Ooorrrr . . . I could teach you how to talk to the babbling brook."

"That sounds fun, too!"

"Oh, oh, or . . . Waitwaitwait! I've got it!" Silvermist somersaulted backward and hovered over a glistening spiderweb. "Dewdrops on spiderwebs!"

Tinker Bell hovered beside Silvermist. She was mesmerized by the web's intricacy. Beautiful drops of dew clung to the delicate strands like jewels. "Ohhhhh!" she exclaimed.

They gazed at the web together, and Silvermist

wiped an admiring tear from her eye. Then she grabbed Tink's arm, eager to get started. "Come on! I'll show you how to do it!"

Fawn waved. "Good luck, Tink!"

Rosetta gave her a wink. "You can do it!"

Iridessa just stood there, obviously waiting for something awful to happen. Fawn and Rosetta gave her an expectant look. "Oh! Um, go . . . get 'em?" she tried. She still looked worried.

Silvermist led Tink to the edge of the pond. "Just cup your hands like this and reach into the water," she said, lifting out a perfect dewdrop. She looked at Tink. "Okay, you've heard of a dewdrop . . . ?" she asked.

Tink nodded.

"This is a *don't* drop," Silvermist finished. Her face was serious, but a mischievous glint sparkled in her eye.

Tink just stared at her. Had Silvermist made a joke? Should she laugh? But she looked so serious!

"That's water-fairy humor," Silvermist said, smiling. Tink heaved a quiet sigh of relief.

Silvermist took her dewdrop and flew to the web, with Tink behind her. "Now, this part can be tricky because it takes a very steady, delicate hand to . . ." She carefully placed the drop on the web. The drop settled, clinging to the thin strand.

Silvermist stared at Tink's empty hands. "Where's *your* dewdrop?"

"Oh!" Tink giggled, embarrassed. She had been so busy watching Silvermist, she had forgotten to try it herself.

Tink flew back to the pond. Slowly and gently, she pulled up a beautiful sparkling drop. "Hey, I did—"

Pop!

The dewdrop burst like a water balloon in her hands. "Oops!"

Silvermist appeared beside her. "Shake that one off! Shake it off! You can do this!"

Tink tried again. She carefully pulled out another drop and began to fly toward the web.

Fawn cheered. "That's it, Tink! You're doing it! You—"

Pop!

The dewdrop burst again.

Tink blew out her breath, lifting her bangs off her forehead. This was harder than it looked. She dipped her hands back into the water.

"Now, Tink," Silvermist began, "try to—"

Pop!

"No, no, sweetie," Silvermist tried again. "You need to—"

Pop!

"Well, maybe if you—"

Pop!

The other fairies winced as Tink failed again and again. They watched her flit back and forth, trying to get each dewdrop to the spiderweb before it burst.

"Well, you have to admire her persistence," Iridessa said grimly.

Tink was so frustrated that she wanted to scream. But she refused to give up. She lifted another drop—a huge one. But instead of trying to carry it, she heaved it toward the web, hoping it would stick before it could burst.

Silvermist, Iridessa, Fawn, and Rosetta watched the giant drop fly through the air and land smack-dab in the middle of the web with a satisfyingly wet *splort!*

But instead of sticking to the web, it bounced off and flew toward Silvermist and the other fairies. *SPLAT!* The dewdrop burst with so much force, it soaked all four of them and knocked Silvermist flat on her back.

Tink hurried to help Silvermist to her feet. She was sorry her friends had gotten wet, but at least she was making some progress. The dewdrop had been on the web, if only for a second! "Should I get another dewdrop?" she asked.

Silvermist shook the water off her wings. Her eyes darted around, finally resting on Iridessa. "You know, Tink," Silvermist said brightly, "you always struck me as a light fairy kind of gal."

Iridessa winced.

Tink knew that Iridessa didn't think her plan was so great, but she still felt optimistic.

Tink smiled happily, determined to ignore the fact that Iridessa was definitely *not* smiling back.

14

*M*eanwhile, at Tinkers' Nook, a tall pile of acorn pails waiting for handles grew higher and higher on Tinker Bell's worktable.

The nature fairies would need every bucket, pail, and basket they could get their hands on. Clank and Bobble worked at a feverish pace. Clank was busy assembling the bodies of the pails and putting them on Tink's worktable so that she could make the handles. Bobble was weaving grass baskets.

It was hard work. Noisy, too. Clank grabbed a couple of wads of flower fluff and stuffed them into his ears. Then he cheerfully began to chop the tops off acorns to make pails. *CHOP! WHAP! CHOP! WHAP! CHOP! WHAP!*

Bobble continued to weave dainty blades of grass into baskets. He glanced over at Tink's table. "Have you seen Tink?" he shouted at Clank.

"No, thank you. Not thirsty!" Clank yelled back. *CHOP! WHAP! CHOP! WHAP! CHOP! WHAP!*

"Not 'drink'!" Bobble yelled over the noise. "Tink!"

"Pink? I like purple m'self!" *CHOP! WHAP! CHOP! WHAP! CHOP! WHAP!*

"Tink!" Bobble bellowed in exasperation. "Have you seen *Tink*?"

Clank stopped, smelled his armpits, and scowled at Bobble. "I do not stink! Maybe it's you."

Clank finished his chopping and pulled the fluff from his ears. He looked over at Tink's worktable and noticed the growing pile of pails to be mended. "Hey, have you seen Tink?" he asked Bobble.

Bobble fought the urge to strangle him and shook his head.

A worried look fell across Clank's face. "Fairy Mary is going to be cross."

Bobble nodded. "Aye, Clank. We'd better take some of this off Miss Bell's plate."

"All right, then."

They flew over to Tink's table. Bobble took a pail from the top of the pile just as Clank pulled one from the bottom.

"No, no, no!" Bobble cried. "Wait, wai—"

But it was too late.

CRASH!

The entire pile came sliding down. Bobble's and Clank's tidy worktables were now covered with mountains of unmended pails.

Unfortunately, Fairy Mary chose that very moment to come flying in.

"Will you two stop mucking about!"

Bobble and Clank each pointed a greasy finger at the other, hoping to escape a scolding. But Fairy Mary's eagle eyes were on Tink's table, which was now completely clear. "I see Tinker Bell has gotten her work done . . . mysteriously. Where is she, anyway?"

Bobble exchanged a nervous look with Clank and they both began talking at once.

"Well, see, she's ah . . . ," Bobble babbled.

Clank talked right over him. "She . . . um . . . she went with Cheese to, uh . . ."

But Cheese was in the corner of the workshop, and when he heard his name, he came right over. He clearly hadn't gone anywhere with anyone.

Fairy Mary's eyes narrowed.

Bobble worked desperately to save the situation. "Uhhhh . . . What Clank means is that she went to get cheese for the mouse because, um, he was whining."

Clank, quick to catch on for once, hurried to back up the story. "Like a baby," he added. The two fairies giggled nervously.

Fairy Mary gave them a long stare that let them know they weren't fooling her. Then she took off.

Bobble let out a sigh of relief. Fairy Mary had let

A fairy is born from a baby's first laugh.
The laugh is carried on a dandelion wisp to Pixie Hollow.

Pixie Hollow is in Never Land.
Here all four seasons exist at once.

Clank and Bobble give Tinker Bell a tour of Pixie Hollow.

Tinker Bell meets many fairies on her first day.
Most of them are friendly, but Vidia is not.

Tinker Bell discovers many strange objects on the beach.

Tink uses some of the strange objects to create a
machine that crushes berries to make paint.

Rosetta, Fawn, Silvermist, and Iridessa reluctantly
agree to help Tink find a new talent.

Iridessa demonstrates how to catch the last
rays of sunlight at dusk.

When Tinker Bell tries to help light the fireflies
for the evening, things don't go as planned.

Tinker Bell is frustrated, but she refuses to give up.

Tink attempts to be an animal fairy. But the baby bird
won't listen to her.

Scout fairies keep watch for hawks, which can eat
a fairy in one bite!

Cheese helps Tinker Bell try to round up the
Sprinting Thistles to prove she is a garden fairy.

Terence wants Tink to realize that she
should be proud of her talent.

Tinker Bell's inventions help save spring, and she
gets to go to the mainland after all.

The music box Tink has fixed makes Wendy Darling very happy.
Being a tinker fairy is wonderful!

them—and Tinker Bell—off the hook this time.

Next time?

Well . . . Fairy Mary wasn't the most forgiving fairy in Never Land.

Bobble hoped Tinker Bell would come back and start tinkering again soon.

They needed her.

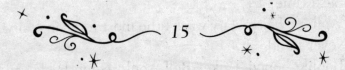

15

*T*ink was happily unaware of the trouble back at the workshop. She was following Iridessa over a meadow full of sunflowers. Several light fairies played jump rope with a beam of light. Others used their glow to create butterfly-shaped shadow puppets.

"Okay, what can I teach you?" Iridessa wondered aloud. "I know! Follow me." She grabbed a bucket from a pile and handed it to Tink. Iridessa gestured at the setting sun. "The last light of day. It's the richest kind of all!"

The beautiful sun set slowly, and the light fairies held their buckets at the ready. Tink could sense their excitement.

"Wait for it. Wait for it," Iridessa cautioned. A streak of warm pink spread across the sky. "Okay . . . aaaaaannd . . . NOW!"

Beams of golden sunlight cascaded down over them. Iridessa cupped her hands to catch the light as Tink held up her bucket.

When Tinker Bell looked down to examine her catch, the bucket was empty.

Iridessa poured some light from her hands into Tink's bucket. It swirled, glimmering like gold. "Incredible!" Tink exclaimed.

"That's just step one," Iridessa said. She finally seemed to be enjoying herself. "Now for the fun part." She led Tink back to the sunflowers. When they reached one particular patch, Iridessa whistled.

Dozens of fireflies with unlit tails were sleeping beneath the sunflowers. But when Iridessa whistled, they woke up. They zigged and zagged around Iridessa and Tink like frisky puppies.

"Okay, okay!" Iridessa reached into Tink's bucket and pulled out some light. The fireflies bounced up and down. Iridessa tossed the light gently into the air and a few fireflies gleefully darted through it to illuminate themselves.

Several unlit fireflies hovered at Tink's feet. They looked up with big, expectant eyes. Tink reached into the bucket and pulled out . . . nothing.

The fireflies whimpered.

Tink felt almost as disappointed as they looked.

Okay. It was time to try harder.

Tink took a deep breath. She reached into the bucket again, concentrating as hard as she possibly could. When she was sure she had a handful of light, she whipped out her fingers and threw . . . nothing!

The fireflies darted off, searching for the light. They returned looking even sadder.

Tink gritted her teeth. Her face contorted into a terrible grimace. She reached into the bucket with so much fury that the fireflies were frightened. They began to slink away.

"STAY!" Tinker Bell snapped.

The fireflies froze.

"Here, Tink," Iridessa said in a calming voice. "Let me." She reached for the bucket.

Tink held it away. "No! I almost got it." She just needed a little more practice. A little more time.

Iridessa tried again. "If I just get you started . . ."

Tinker Bell's fingers ached from the effort. "AAARGH! This is impossible!" She angrily threw the bucket to the ground.

Bang!

Streaks of golden light shot out in every direction.

"LOOK OUT!" Iridessa shrieked.

The fireflies snapped into action, chasing after the light while all the light fairies ducked for cover.

One beam ricocheted off a rock and then came careening back. It hit Tink square in the backside. "Oh, no!" she cried.

Tink peeked at her behind. It glowed as brightly as the rear end of a firefly. How absolutely mortifying!

The fireflies stopped and stared. Then every single one of them zoomed straight toward Tink, clearly thinking she was the biggest, prettiest firefly they had ever seen.

Tinker Bell flapped her wings and flew as fast as she could, trying to escape the lovesick swarm.

"Fly, Tink, fly!" Iridessa yelled.

"We'll save you, Tink!" Fawn shouted.

But Tink couldn't wait for help. The last thing she heard as she sped away was Rosetta shouting, "Cover your tushieeeeeeee!"

16

By the next morning, the glow had worn off Tink's backside. Her happy optimism had worn away, too.

She sat in the workshop feeling glum while Clank and Bobble worked and murmured their song.

"Fiddle and fix, craft and create—"

"—carve acorn buckets, to hold flower paint."

"When preparing for spring, we do all this and more."

"Yes, being a tinker is never a bore!"

Tinker Bell was too unhappy to join in. She let out a long sigh as she did her best to mend a kettle.

Fairy Mary came flying over and landed next to Tink. "I'd like a word with you," she said.

Tink tried not to look as guilty as she felt. "Fairy Mary!" she cried in a casual, breezy tone, as if she were just the fairy she had been hoping to meet. "See, I was on my deliveries," she improvised, "and . . . uh . . . It's actually kind of a funny story. . . ."

"Save it," Fairy Mary snapped. "I know what you've been up to, missy!"

Tinker Bell froze.

"And I had such high hopes for you." Fairy Mary looked genuinely disappointed. As she flew away, Tink began to feel even worse. She was just trying to be the best fairy she could be. So why did Fairy Mary have to make her feel so guilty about it?

Tinker Bell glared at the litter of pots and pans on her worktable.

"You'd do well to listen to her, Miss Bell," Bobble said.

"Why?" Tinker Bell demanded bitterly. "So I can do this my whole life? I don't want to be just a—a— stupid tinker."

Clank and Bobble looked shocked . . . and hurt.

Tink saw their stricken faces and began to stutter an apology, trying to take the words back. "I—I didn't mean . . ."

But the damage was done. Both of them stared at her with sad eyes.

Clank and Bobble silently returned to their work.

"I . . . I have to go," she said to their stiff backs.

Tinker Bell bolted out the window. She would make it up to them later, she told herself. She didn't know how exactly, but she would figure it out.

Right now she had more important things to do.

And Fawn was waiting.

17

By the time Tink arrived at Pine Tree Grove, the animal fairies were hard at work. Tink watched as Fawn coaxed a baby bird to fly for the very first time.

After a few minutes of petting and reassurance from Fawn, the little bird stepped up to the edge of the nest and took the plunge. He flew clumsily but happily. Fawn followed behind, calling out cheerful encouragements.

Scout fairies in their pinecone watchtowers scanned the skies with leaf-and-dewdrop binoculars, ready to sound a warning at the first hint of danger.

Tink flew over to join Fawn, who gave her a smile. "Hey, Tink! You ready?"

"I'm a little nervous, actually," Tink admitted.

Fawn laughed. "Oh, don't be silly. You'll be fine. We're teaching baby birds how to fly."

Fawn led Tink back to the nest. Another hatchling watched them with big eyes. "First, you have to get their attention," Fawn explained. "Then smile, and establish trust." Fawn gave the bird a sweet grin and a pat on the head. "See?"

The tiny chick twittered bashfully and hopped up to get a better look at Fawn.

"Okay," Fawn said to the little bird. "Flap your wings. That's right. Up and down. Up and down. Like this." Fawn flapped her wings, and the baby bird flapped his, mimicking her.

Fawn applauded. "That's the way. Now faster, faster. That's right!"

The little bird began to rise into the air.

"Yes! You're doing it! Okay, come out this way a bit." Little by little, Fawn coaxed the bird forward. When he looked down and realized he was in the air, he began to drop, but Fawn skillfully boosted him back up. "Oops! You're okay! You're okay!"

The bird grew more confident but dipped again. Fawn stayed right behind him. "Keep flapping. Just keep flapping!" she cried. "Why don't you help that last little guy?" she shouted to Tink.

Tink looked into the nest and spotted a tiny chick hunkered down low. He was clearly hoping not to be seen. "Smile and establish trust," Tink reminded herself.

She gave him a big grin. Too big, maybe. Instead of a friendly cheep, the baby bird greeted her with a terrified squawk.

Tinker Bell tried not to take it personally. "Hey, little fellow. You want to do some flap-flap today?"

The bird shook his head.

"Oh, sure you do!" Tink said brightly. "All you do is just flap your wings, like this." Tinker Bell began to rise, hoping the little bird would follow along. But when she looked down to check his progress, he was hiding behind the shards of his eggshell.

"Oh, no! None of that." Tink tried to pull him out from behind the eggshell. "Come on. All we've got to do is—ouch!" The hatchling had given her hand a hard peck.

Tink narrowed her eyes. Okay. It looked as if she was going to have to do this the hard way.

Tinker Bell lunged at the little bird. But he stepped aside and Tink hit the other side of the nest headfirst.

CRASH!

"Phhhht!" Tink spit out a mouthful of nesting twigs and feathers. She stared at the hatchling. The hatchling stared stubbornly back. Tink was going to have to get tough.

"Look," she said between clenched teeth. "I'm going to level with you, okay? I kind of bombed on the whole water- and light-fairy things. I'm starting to run out of options here. So if you'd flap your little wings and take flight for a few measly seconds, I might be able to go to the mainland and bring happiness to the world! Whaddya say?"

The bird reached for a piece of eggshell and slowly began to reassemble his shell—around himself.

Tink exploded. "Wrong answer!" She grabbed the chick's wings and pulled. One way or another, this cute little birdie was going to leave the nest. "If I end up making acorn kettles for the rest of my life, I'm holding you personally responsible! OW! OW! OW!"

The bird pecked frantically at Tink's hands and face.

"Stop squirming! OW! HEY! OW! OKAY, FINE! I'M LETTING GO!" Tink released him and looked around for Fawn. This was not working. She was going to need some help.

All the animal fairies seemed to be busy. But up in the sky, silhouetted against the sun, she saw a huge bird soaring majestically.

Tink perked up. "Maybe that guy can help!" she said to the little bird. "He's a really good flier."

Tink shot up into the air, streaking toward the bird. "Hey! Hey, up there!"

Higher and higher she flew. So high that she didn't hear the voices of the scout fairies. She looked down. They all seemed to be watching her. Waving their arms. Shaking their heads. Trying desperately to tell her something.

Whatever it was, it would have to wait. This bird was traveling fast. If Tink didn't get his attention, he'd be gone.

Tinker Bell put her hands around her mouth and yelled as loudly as she could at the bird.

The big bird turned and began flying back toward Tink. All right! It had worked.

But then Tink got a good look at the bird, now diving directly at her, and her heart came to an awful, sickening stop.

It was a hawk!

18

Thinking fast, Tink dove straight down. She aimed for the dense branches. Maybe if she disappeared into the foliage she could lose the hawk.

She flew into the canopy of the woods. The leaves slapped briskly at her arms and legs as they closed behind her.

CRRAACK!

She could hear the hawk swooping through the branches behind her.

Tink spied a knothole in a tree trunk. She headed for it, zigging and zagging. She dove inside and cowered against the inner wall of the hollow trunk just in time. Outside, the hawk screamed and clawed at the bark.

Suddenly, someone pulled her wings down and spun her around.

"Vidia!"

"This is *my* hiding spot!" the fast-flying fairy hissed.

There was a hideous cracking sound and they both screamed. The hawk had torn a big chunk of bark away from the knothole. It wouldn't be long before he was able to reach in with his talons.

Vidia ran toward a hole in the floor of the trunk. "It's all yours now." And with that, she jumped into the opening and disappeared.

Tink followed her.

The two fairies slid through the chute in the trunk of the tree. Tink could see the light at the end of the hole.

Just ahead of Tink, Vidia came to a screeching stop, grabbing the edges of the knothole to keep from sliding out.

Tink tried to grab hold of something herself, but she wasn't quick enough. She skidded right into Vidia, sending the raven-haired fairy sprawling out onto a branch—right between the taloned feet of the hawk!

Vidia looked up, her eyes widening with horror. The hawk looked down and opened his beak to strike.

At that moment, a hail of rocks, twigs, berries, and seeds showered over the hawk. The bird reared back.

A second volley of rocks and sticks rained down over his head. He veered from side to side, disoriented.

"Get him!"

"Go on!"

"Get out of here!"

Tink could hear the fairies shouting at the hawk as they pelted him with anything and everything they could get their hands on.

Finally, the hawk wheeled upward and flew away. His angry screech echoed through the forest, raising the hair on the back of every fairy neck in Pixie Hollow.

The fairies gathered around Vidia. She was a mess. She had gotten hit with a few berries herself and was covered with bits of pulp and purple juice.

Some giggled, but Tink actually felt sorry for her. Haughty Vidia, the fastest fairy in Pixie Hollow, looked bedraggled, defeated, rattled, and humiliated. Tink approached her carefully.

"You have a little . . ." She reached out to try to wipe the berry juice from Vidia's cheek.

Vidia pushed her hand away. "No touching!" she snapped. "I'm fine."

"But I was only trying to help."

"Well, stop trying." Vidia scrambled to her feet and flew away, looking even more fierce than the hawk, and a lot more purple.

Silvermist, Rosetta, Iridessa, and Fawn gathered around Tink. "Tinker Bell—" Silvermist began.

Tink cut her off. There was nothing anybody could say now that would make her feel better.

Everything she did was a disaster. "I can't hold water," she said. "Can't hold light. Birds hate me. I'm just so . . . so useless!"

"Tink—" Fawn began.

Tink spread her wings and flew away.

"We have to go help her," she heard Silvermist say.

But Tink knew that nobody could help her.

19

*T*ink flew to the beach cove to sulk. She settled down on the sand and began chucking pebbles into the foliage while she muttered to herself.

"Great. I failed for the third time in a row. At this rate, I should get to the mainland right around . . . oh, never." She angrily heaved a pebble and heard an unexpected *clink!*

Curiosity won out over self-pity. Tinker Bell flew over to see what was in the underbrush. She pulled aside the leaves and emerged into a little clearing.

In the middle of the clearing stood a mysterious machine . . . or what was left of one.

A round porcelain box encased the machine. Tink peered inside at an intricate arrangement of springs and levers—most of them out of place, bent, or broken.

She couldn't help smiling. Rust and water had done a lot of damage. But it was still a lovely thing— and it would be a *beautiful* thing when she got through with it.

Tink cracked her knuckles and got right to work.

She enjoyed putting the pieces together like a puzzle. Little by little, the apparatus began to take shape. Tinker Bell tweaked this and twisted that, using imagination and ingenuity to make it work. Flat-sided seashells made great screwdrivers. Seaweed made a terrific polishing cloth. And jellyfish jelly made excellent grease.

Before long, she had repaired a strange metal comb, using twigs and pine-needle tips. She plucked the tines of the comb, listening to the different musical note each one made.

Finally, all the parts were back inside the box and in their correct places. The gears were tight, and each screw was snug. The metal comb was fastened into its slot, with the tines lined up against a mysterious cylinder with little bumps all over it. Now, if only Tinker Bell knew what the box did!

Tink closed the lid. As she did, she noticed a hole in the lid that led directly into the gears of the box. There must be one more part, Tink realized. She looked around and noticed a brass post sticking out of a nearby bush. As she pulled the post out, she saw that it was attached to the feet of a porcelain dancer. The figure was about Tink's size.

Using a sprinkle of pixie dust to make the dancer light, Tink managed to carry her to the box and restore her to her rightful place on the very top. The post at her feet fit perfectly into the hole in the lid.

Tinker Bell took the dancer's outstretched hand and slowly spun her around. The most astonishing thing happened as the dancer turned: the box began to play a melody! Oh, it was so beautiful! Tink's heart swelled. *Now I need a name for it,* she thought, and wracked her brain for a name. "Melody machine"? "Ditty player"? *Oh, well,* she thought, *"music box" will have to do until I come up with something better.*

A sudden burst of applause startled her. She whirled around and saw Rosetta, Fawn, Iridessa, and Silvermist watching, beaming with pride.

"You fixed it!" Silvermist exclaimed.

"Amazing!" Rosetta sighed.

"What are you guys doing here?" Tink cried.

But her friends were too busy admiring the music box to answer.

"Wow! That is beautiful!" Fawn said.

Iridessa's eyes were opened wide. "It might be the sparkliest thing I've ever seen. And I've seen a lot of sparkly things!"

Silvermist flew slowly around the box. "It's a really pretty, uh . . . thingy. What is it?"

Tinker Bell rubbed the end of her nose. "I don't know. I just found it."

Rosetta smiled and glowed even pinker than

usual. "Tinker Bell, do you realize what you're doing? You're tinkering!"

Tinker Bell shook her head forcefully. Fixing the music box hadn't felt at all like putting handles on acorn pails. It had been fun. Fun like inventing the nutcracker and the flower-sprayer. "No, this isn't . . . I was just—"

Rosetta stopped her. "Creating those gadgets, figuring things out, fixing stuff like this . . . that's what tinkering is, sweetie!"

Iridessa's glow flickered emphatically. "Don't you like doing this? Isn't it what you really love?"

Her friends had a point, Tink had to admit. If this was really what tinkering was about, then she certainly couldn't claim she didn't love it.

"Yeah!" Silvermist said. "Who cares about going to the mainland, anyway?"

That was when Tinker Bell recalled why she didn't want to be a tinker. "Well, *I* do, remember?" She gestured at the music box. "I want to see where these things come from! Are you just giving up on me?" She turned to look at Rosetta. "I mean, aren't you going to teach me how to be a garden fairy anymore?"

Rosetta took a step forward. "Oh, sweetpea, I think *this* is your talent."

Silvermist shook her head, and droplets of water

flew from the ends of her hair. "Tink, we just want you to be happy."

Somehow, that just made Tink angrier. "If you really wanted to help, you'd help me get to the mainland like you promised."

Fawn reached out her hand. "Please, Tink. Just think about it."

Tink backed away. What was there to think about? Sure, she liked to tinker. So what? What good was it if it didn't help her get what she wanted?

Her friends exchanged sad and helpless looks. Tink could see that they finally understood that nothing they could say or do was going to change her feelings. The four fairies rose into the air.

Tink watched them fly away. High overhead, visible even in the day, was the Second Star—a signpost pointing to a destination she would never see. Why? Because she was a failure.

If her friends wouldn't help her, then she was out of options.

Unless . . .

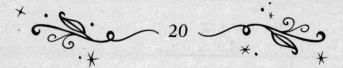

20

*L*ater that night, Tink flew toward Vidia's house, which was in a lone sour-plum tree perched on the edge of a craggy slope.

Vidia opened the door. Her eyes grew wide when she saw Tinker Bell.

Tink gave her a pleading smile. "Will you teach me how to be a fast-flying fairy?"

Vidia answered by slamming the door in Tink's face.

Tink knocked insistently. "Pleeeeease?" she begged. "I know I could do it. With your help, I could be flying as fast as you in no time."

There was no answer.

Tink slumped against the door. "Vidia!" she begged. "You're my last hope. All my so-called friends have given up on me. Rosetta won't even try to teach me how to be a garden fairy now."

Still no answer. Tink went on, mostly talking to herself. "I bet I could at least paint some flowers, or round up some sproutlings—there must be something I can do—"

The door opened. Tink jumped, startled. Vidia stood there with her arms crossed and a sly smile on her face.

"Or . . . ," Vidia said sweetly, "if you *really* wanted to be a garden fairy . . ."

21

Needlepoint Meadow was deserted. Rogue breezes blew in every direction, tossing Tink's hair as she put the finishing touches on the corral she had built out of twigs. It had high walls and a sturdy gate. She stepped back to admire it.

Tink didn't like what Vidia had suggested. But she had to admit it was a good idea—if she could pull it off.

If Vidia's plan worked, Tink would be the first fairy in the history of Pixie Hollow to capture the Sprinting Thistles. No one could argue she didn't have garden talent after that!

Suddenly, Tink caught a glimpse of something running past her. When she tried to see what it was, it disappeared into the landscape.

Then something ran the other way.

Again, she turned her head.

Again, she saw nothing.

This place was giving her the creeps. Cheese was scared, too. He cowered in the back of the corral.

"Oh, come on—they're just weeds!" Tink scolded the mouse, trying to make him—and herself—feel braver.

Tink flew up and settled into the saddle on Cheese's back. She tested a flaxen lasso, twirling it with ease. "Besides, there were only seven or eight at the most. Right?" She snapped the reins, but Cheese didn't budge.

"We can do this," she said firmly, forcing him out into the meadow. They galloped over the grass, going faster and faster.

A couple of Thistles popped up from their hiding places and ran.

Aha!

Tink and Cheese maneuvered around the Thistles. Tink guided them toward the corral with some twigs she had fashioned into prods.

It worked like a charm. "All right! Hi-yah! Git! Git! Come on!"

Two more Thistles rose from their hiding places, and they all ran into the corral. "It's working!" Tinker Bell shouted happily. She slammed the corral's gate, closing the Thistles in. Then she and Cheese quickly galloped back into the meadow to find more Thistles.

Tink never noticed Vidia, who flew up and spun around the corral, creating a whirlwind that blew the gate open.

The Thistles ran out of the gate just as Tink came galloping back, driving a new group toward the corral. "Wait, wait, wait! Wrong way!" she shouted at the runaways.

They rushed right past her, breaking her twig-prods. Ten more Thistles popped up and joined the herd.

By now, the pitter-patter of Thistle feet was turning into a rumble. Tink began to get a bad feeling.

She looked back over her shoulder, and her eyes grew large with horror.

There were hundreds of Thistles now—all galloping toward her!

Tink tried to swallow her panic. "At least they're all headed toward the corral," she said to Cheese. She raised her voice and shouted at the herd. "Please file into the corral in an orderly manner!"

CRASHHH!

The Thistles washed over the tiny corral like a tidal wave, and the carefully constructed fence collapsed into a pile of splinters.

Tink twirled her lasso over her head and took off after the Thistles at full gallop. "Waaaiiiit! Come baaaack!"

But they weren't listening. The Thistle stampede flooded down the path. Tink's heart sank into her pom-pommed slippers when she realized where they were going. They were heading toward Springtime Square!

"Oh, no!" Tinker Bell shouted. "Come on!" she cried, urging Cheese.

Cheese leaped forward, and he and Tinker Bell pounded along the path of destruction the Thistles had left behind them.

22

The Thistles thundered through Sunflower Meadow. Tinker Bell and Cheese followed close behind. As they tried to catch up to the stampede, Tink spared a glance around her.

Light fairies and fireflies had scattered in every direction, leaping for cover and clinging to the undersides of the tall flowers. The Thistles had sheared off low-hanging petals and leaves. The fireflies were trembling, their glows winked out from fright.

"Sorry . . . sorry . . . 'scuse me . . . ," Tink said.

The Thistles kept running. They were heading toward Lilypad Pond, where the water fairies were happily showering their lilies. The fairies had no idea what lay in store for them.

RRRRUMBLE! The Thistles charged through Lilypad Pond, knocking lilies over and scattering water fairies in every direction. Tink and Cheese hopped over the remaining lily pads. Fairies glared at her in shocked outrage from every corner of the pond. "Sorry!" Tink cried, wishing she could stay to help clean up.

But the Thistles were already charging toward the Flower Garden, where flower fairies watched with pride as rows of little bulbs awaited inspection.

"Okay," a flower fairy said to her charges. "Come on, little ones—" She broke off with a cry of alarm as the Thistles came thundering through.

The baby bulbs scattered. Some ran for cover on their rooty feet. Others dug holes in the ground and jumped inside before the Thistles could run them over.

Up ahead in Flutterby Forest, dozens of freshly painted ladybugs were waiting for their final spots. "We're almost done!" an art fairy was saying. "This is the last batch." Then she looked up at the Thistles coming right for her. "Oh, no!"

By now, Tinker Bell couldn't have stopped Cheese if she wanted to. The mouse was determined to stay on the trail of the Thistles. They rode through a cloud of terrified ladybugs, heading straight for Springtime Square, where the huge collection of spring supplies was waiting.

The square was filled with carefully stacked pots of paint, bundles of seeds, baskets of bulbs, and sacks of pollen. Every fairy had worked her and his hardest for months to get to this point—ready for spring.

Rosetta, Fawn, Iridessa, and Silvermist were standing with a group of nature fairies, admiring the preparations, when they looked up and saw disaster sweeping toward them.

"Oh, no—the spring supplies!"

"Not the flower paint!"

"Save the seeds!"

"The pollen, the pollen!"

But there was nothing anyone could do.

The awful Thistle stampede thundered through Springtime Square, destroying everything in its path.

23

By the time the stampede broke up, the wreckage was complete.

Every basket and bucket was broken.

Seeds, paint, light, and scared little bulbs lay strewn everywhere.

Fireflies had flickered out in fear.

Ladybugs were splattered with every color of paint.

And dazed nature fairies wandered around the devastation trying to take in what had just happened.

When Clank and Bobble flew in and saw the mess, their eyes welled up with tears.

The Minister of Spring picked up a surviving flower, but it wilted in his hand.

Tinker Bell and Cheese slowed to a stop in the middle of the square. Tink slid off Cheese's back and stood on shaking legs. "Oh, no." Her voice was empty and hollow-sounding.

"What happened?" Fawn asked quietly.

Iridessa's hands were pressed against her mouth. She was too shocked to even make a comment.

"Tinker Bell! What did you think you were doing?" Rosetta's voice was sharp. It was the first time Tinker Bell had heard her sound angry.

"I was just trying to . . . I thought if I could corral the Thistles . . ." She trailed off, realizing how totally thoughtless she had been.

Rosetta exploded. "There isn't a garden fairy alive who can control those weeds! What were you trying to prove?"

"She's right, Tink. This has all gone too far." Silvermist's voice was gentle but very firm.

Queen Clarion came swirling into their midst in a bright, glittering cloud of pixie dust. Her face turned pale as she looked around, taking in the full scope of the disaster. "By the Second Star!" she exclaimed. "All the preparations for spring . . . How did this happen?"

Silvermist put a protective hand on Tink's arm.

Tink was grateful, but she knew no one could help her now. She gently pulled her arm away and approached the queen with her heart pounding in her chest. "Queen Clarion, it was me. I did it. It was all my fault."

There were gasps from the crowd, and some groans.

Queen Clarion raised her hands to her cheeks.

"Tinker Bell . . ." The queen's voice trailed off.

But Tink couldn't defend her own silly and selfish behavior now. "I'm sorry," she finally managed to choke out.

Then she took to the air so that she wouldn't have to see the sad and disappointed eyes of her friends.

24

That evening, at sunset, the Council of Seasons met in a cavernous chamber high in the Pixie Dust Tree.

Gathered there, among the leaf books and scrolls, were Queen Clarion, her four season ministers, and Fairy Mary.

"I don't think we can fix this in time," said the Minister of Spring. "And if we're not ready when the Everblossom opens, we're going to have to cancel spring, or postpone it at the very least."

"And put my snowflake fairies back to work? Oh, no!" argued the Minister of Winter.

The Minister of Summer, with eyes as green as grass, shook her head. "We can't! We can't do that! If the snow isn't melted, the seedlings won't grow, our fruit won't ripen in the summer and . . ."

". . . and in the fall, there will be nothing to harvest," the Minister of Autumn finished for her. "Spring must happen on time, or the balance of nature will be undone!"

"There must be something we can do," the Minister of Winter insisted. "Certainly this has happened before!"

"It has!" the Minister of Spring snapped. "Did you ever hear of the Ice Age?"

Queen Clarion lifted her hands, asking for calm. "Settle down, all of you. Fairy Mary, is it even possible to redo everything in such a short time?"

With a flick of her finger, Fairy Mary sent the last birdseed bead spinning across the abacus. Her calculations were complete.

"No," she said as the bead made a loud and final *clack!*

"We were so close," mourned the Minister of Spring. "And now it's all gone."

"Who will paint the leaves now?" the Minister of Summer asked.

"The apples and pumpkins will never grow," the Minister of Autumn groaned.

The Minister of Spring dabbed at his eyes. "It took months to harvest all those seeds."

The Minister of Winter shook her beautiful head. "Every season is going to suffer."

Queen Clarion and Fairy Mary said nothing at all. The situation was just too awful for words.

25

Meanwhile, far below the council chamber, Tink sat alone by the Pixie Dust Well, listening to the angry voices echoing overhead.

How had things gone so wrong so fast?

A tear streaked down her cheek and fell into the glowing well.

The sound of a footfall startled Tink, and she spun around. A figure emerged out of the dark. It was Terence, the handsome dust-keeper. "You okay, Tink?"

"I'm fine," she lied. "I just came hoping to get a quick refill. I'm going away for a while."

"Oh? How long will you be gone?" Terence flew over to the well and dipped his ladle in.

There was no point in lying, Tink realized. They'd all know soon enough. And she doubted anyone would try to stop her from going. "Well, actually, forever."

Terence was taken aback, but he tried to hide it. "Forever? Well, in that case . . ." He dipped his ladle extra deep and brought it up heaping with dust. "You'll need a double scoop. Forever's a pretty long time, so I hear." He poured the dust over Tink's shoulders and wings, making them glitter and shine.

Tinker Bell smiled. "Thanks, Terence." His were the first kind words she had heard in a while, and she felt a lump rise in her throat.

"You know my name?" He sounded surprised.

"Well, sure. Why wouldn't I?"

"I don't know. I'm just a dust-keeper. Not exactly the most important fairy in Pixie Hollow."

"What are you talking about?" Tink replied. She was shocked to hear Terence describe himself in such lowly terms. "You're probably the most important one there is! Without you, no one would have any magic!"

Terence considered that for a moment and smiled. But Tink wasn't done yet.

"Why, your talent makes you who you are," she went on. "You should be proud of it!"

"*I* am," Terence said, looking at Tink meaningfully.

Tink's mouth fell open in surprise. No, she wasn't proud of herself right now. In fact, she was ashamed. But she wasn't ashamed because of what her talent was, she was ashamed because . . . "I'd better get going," she said quickly.

26

*T*hat night, while the moonbeams played across the empty workshop of Tinkers' Nook, Tinker Bell was still thinking about Terence's words.

She had been certain that the best thing she could do for Pixie Hollow was to leave.

But what if she was wrong—again?

Tinker Bell walked through the workshop, looking at the litter of tools, pots, kettles, and buckets. So many things to be mended. So many things to be made. So much to be done.

Her fingers itched to take up a tool and begin working again. She smiled. How funny. After all her complaining, it turned out that she really did love tinkering.

She felt something nuzzle her hand. "Hey, Cheese," she said quietly. She petted his head, still looking around.

Over in one corner, she spotted her useless inventions. All her shame and doubt came pouring back. "Be proud of your talent," she muttered to herself sarcastically. "What talent? I couldn't even get these silly things to work."

She turned. A beam of moonlight streaming through the window reflected off something in the other corner of the room. Intrigued, Tink went to investigate. She pulled a tarp aside and gasped. "The Lost Things!"

Piled underneath the tarp were all the things she had found. Fairy Mary had said her treasures were rubbish, but they still fascinated Tink.

She picked up a tiny brass screw and admired its smooth, shiny surface and its even grooves. Tink's eyes darted back and forth between the screw and her inventions. She looked at the way the screw was made, how the spiraling threads might help fasten pieces together.

Suddenly, she had an idea.

Not just one idea—a bunch of ideas. Her heart started to race.

"That's it!" she cried.

There wasn't much time.

She would have to hurry.

27

*I*t was deep into the night by the time Tink pulled her wagon up to the edge of Springtime Square. Queen Clarion and Fairy Mary came flying to the square, followed by the Ministers of the Seasons.

All the fairies in Pixie Hollow were gathered. Many were still trying to clean up the square. Others were waiting to hear what the council had decided.

"Attention, everyone!" Queen Clarion called out. "Attention."

The fairies fell silent.

"I'm afraid I have distressing news. There is no way spring can come on time."

The fairies groaned, but Queen Clarion continued. "Months of work were lost, and it will take us months to restore it all. So when the Everblossom opens . . ." The crowd looked up at the huge flower, poised to announce the arrival of spring. ". . . I'm afraid we will not be going to the mainland for spring."

Into the stunned silence, Tink shouted, "Wait!"

She soared out of the wagon and landed lightly in front of Queen Clarion and Fairy Mary. In her hands was her new and improved berry-paint sprayer, with a mainland-style crank.

"I know how we can fix everything!" Tinker Bell insisted breathlessly.

Vidia, standing among the assembled fairies, made a loud scoffing sound.

A few fairies laughed; some murmured angrily.

But not all of them.

Not her friends.

And not the tinkers.

"Tinker Bell," said Queen Clarion, "I don't think this is the—"

"Just hear me out! Please!" Tink begged. She held up her first invention.

Tinker Bell turned to a painting fairy who stood next to an all-red ladybug. "How long does it take you to paint a ladybug?" Tink asked.

"I don't know," the fairy answered. "Ten or fifteen minutes, I guess?"

Tink aimed the berry-paint sprayer at the ladybug and fired.

"No!" the painting fairy shouted. But to her utter amazement, the sprayer instantly painted a perfect pattern of black dots on the ladybug's back.

The painting fairy smiled, pleasantly surprised, as

did the bug. The crowd murmured again, but this time it was with interest, not anger.

Tink reached into her tunic and pulled out a leaf scroll covered with designs. "We can build more of these. I can show you how. Making paint, gathering seeds—we can do it all in no time!" she exclaimed. "We at least have to try!"

The fairies peered at the designs and whispered. Hope began to lift their spirits.

Vidia made an impatient noise and turned to the crowd of fairies. "Are we really going to listen to her? She's the reason we're in this mess in the first place!"

"But I can fix it!" Tinker Bell insisted.

Vidia snorted. "Oh, yippee!" she said sarcastically. "Tinker Bell's going to save us with her dopey little doohickeys! Hide the squirrels!"

Tink felt anger rising in her chest. "What is your problem, Vidia? Why do you think you're so much better than me?"

"I *am* better than you, sweetie," Vidia shot back. "I didn't ruin spring!"

"At least now I'm trying to help," Tink snapped. "Have you ever helped anyone besides yourself?"

Vidia's eyes narrowed. "Well, I tried to help you! Maybe I should have told you to capture the hawk instead of the Thistles!" As soon as the words were out of her mouth, Vidia realized her mistake.

There was a loud gasp from the crowd as they grasped the meaning of what Vidia had just said. Chasing the Thistles had been Vidia's idea. She had put Tink up to it, knowing that Tink was too new, and too inexperienced, to understand the danger.

Vidia's face turned pale. She shut her mouth with a snap and shot a nervous glance toward Queen Clarion.

There was a hushed silence.

Queen Clarion gave Vidia a stern and knowing look. "Perhaps Tinker Bell was not the only one responsible," she said. "Your fast-flying talent is well suited to chasing down each and every one of the Thistles."

Vidia's tightly closed mouth fell open. "Me?"

"Yes. And I expect them all to be returned to Needlepoint Meadow as soon as possible."

"But . . . but that could take forever!" Vidia protested.

"Then I suggest you get started," Queen Clarion replied coolly.

Tinker Bell watched Vidia fly away angrily.

But Tink didn't enjoy seeing Vidia humiliated. She couldn't. No matter what Vidia had or hadn't done, it was Tink who had set the disaster in motion, and it was Tink who needed to put things right.

Queen Clarion turned to her. "Now, Tinker Bell,

are you sure you can do this?" she asked.

Tink directed her words to Queen Clarion, but she was really speaking to Clank and Bobble, her friends whose feelings she had hurt so badly. "Yes. Because I'm a tinker. It's who I am. And tinkers fix things."

Clank and Bobble exchanged a happy look.

"But I can't do it alone!" Tink added.

"Command us, Miss Bell!" Clank and Bobble said in unison. They flew to her side and saluted.

Silvermist, Iridessa, Fawn, and Rosetta also rose out of the crowd and joined Clank and Bobble. "We'll help, too!" Silvermist promised.

"Show us how, Tink!" said Fawn.

Rosetta's voice was sweet again. "I'll help you."

Even Iridessa glowed with excitement. "Me too!"

Tinker Bell grinned from ear to ear, but one look at Fairy Mary's face reminded her that there was work to be done.

"Okay, gather up all the twigs you can, all different sizes. And twine. And tree sap. We'll need lots of that. But most importantly . . ." She tried hard to avoid Fairy Mary's eyes. She knew she was right about this. ". . . we need to find Lost Things."

28

The fairies searched high and low throughout Pixie Hollow. They found Lost Things everywhere, and they brought them all back to Tinker Bell for inspection.

Tink pored over each and every one. A fork. A spoon. A hinge. A mousetrap. A fishing lure. An antique fountain pen. An old leather glove. And a strange apparatus that one of the music fairies told them was called a harmonica.

It wasn't long before Tink had figured out how to make a huge berry/nut squasher. The other fairies gathered around, eager to help her construct it.

"Twig," Tinker Bell said, holding out her hand like a surgeon demanding a scalpel.

A nature fairy placed a twig in her waiting palm. Tink attached it to the acorn and held out her hand again. "Hammer."

A tinker fairy hurried to give her one. Tink used it to tap the twig into place.

"Boingy thingy."

Clank pulled the spring from his pocket and gave it to Tinker Bell. She looked at it and rubbed her chin. "Actually, I need the pointy metal doohickey."

Bobble handed her the fork. "No. Not that one."

Someone else offered her the fishing lure. "Ew! Not that one."

Finally, someone handed her a gear. "Yes! That one!" Tink took it and quickly tied it into place. "Magnification, please."

A light fairy held a pair of eyeglasses in front of the apparatus so that Tink could see it nice and big through the lenses. "And that's how you do it," Tink said to the crowd of fairies watching her work.

Minutes later, they had a machine with a dozen berry/nut squashers in a row. "Put the berries in," Tink instructed, "and we'll have plenty of paint in no time."

The berry-picking fairies dumped berries into the squashers, turned the wheel, and cheered when a dozen buckets filled up with paint.

Painting fairies poured the paint into their new and improved berry-paint sprayers and got to work painting ladybugs.

The next big problem Tink had to tackle was cleaning up the spilled seeds. How could the fairies gather them into baskets as quickly as possible? She looked around— Aha!

At Tink's bidding, two fairies picked up an old work glove and followed her toward a perfume bottle. With a tweak and a twist and a shove and a tap, Tink soon had the harmonica wedged into the opening of the glove. *Snip! Snip!* She quickly cut off the fingertips.

Tinker Bell attached the perfume bottle to the thumb of the glove. "You just squeeze this . . . ," Tink explained. She used the rubber bulb on the perfume bottle to suck air out of the glove. That, in turn, sucked in the seeds that had been lying near the cut-off fingers.

As the glove refilled with air, the seeds were spit out through the harmonica and into waiting baskets.

The contraption was noisy, but it did the job. Soon a team of fairies was flying along with the device, which was busily honking and huffing and picking up seeds.

Tink grinned. "See? Simple!"

Iridessa applauded. "It's working!" the light fairy cried in amazement. "It's working!"

Tink was thrilled. Supplies were piling up so fast, the bird carriers could hardly keep up. The Minister of Spring went through leaf scroll after leaf scroll as he listed the inventory.

Tink spread her wings and flew up to get an aerial view of their progress. Her heart swelled. There were baskets, buckets, and bugs as far as the eye could see.

She cast an anxious glance at the Everblossom. Would they have enough supplies to deliver spring to the mainland by the time the flower opened?

Tink hurried back down to help. Time was of the essence. Every second counted. So did every seed. And so did every fairy.

29

By dawn, the fairies were exhausted but hopeful. Never in the entire history of Pixie Hollow had so much work been completed so quickly.

The Minister of Spring clapped his hands. "Form up, everyone! Look sharp, now!"

Garden fairies gathered up baskets of seeds and buckets of berry paint. Animal fairies saddled up birds. Flower bulbs and ladybugs piled into their containers.

Tink looked up and saw Queen Clarion arriving just as the light from the rising sun began to illuminate the Everblossom.

Magically, the petals of the Everblossom opened and lit Springtime Square with a soft golden glow.

The fairies cheered as the queen landed and looked around the square with pride.

Her eyes missed nothing, and when they fell on Tinker Bell's face, she stretched out her hand. "You did it, Tinker Bell! You saved spring!"

"No," Tinker Bell insisted. "We *all* did it."

Tinker Bell's friends rushed to hug her.

"Queen Clarion," Silvermist begged sweetly. "Can't Tink come with us to the mainland?"

"She's done so much for everyone," Fawn added.

Tinker Bell shook her head. "No. Really. It's okay. I don't need to go."

Rosetta fluttered her lashes in confusion. "But, buttercup, it's what you wanted."

"It's okay," Tink repeated. "My work is here. And I still have a lot of work to do."

"Not here, you don't!" countered a loud and bossy voice.

Fairy Mary came elbowing through the crowd with a very serious look on her face.

Tink gulped. How had she managed to get herself in trouble again?

Fairy Mary turned her head and whistled.

At her signal, Clank and Bobble led Cheese and the wagon into the middle of the square. Sitting in the back was the beautiful music box.

Tinker Bell's mouth fell open in surprise.

Someone had finished cleaning the box, and it sparkled like a jewel.

Bobble's eyes goggled happily. "Surprise, Miss Bell!" he shouted.

"We found your tiny dancer," Clank said with a grin.

Fairy Mary came to stand beside Tink. "I actually ran across this myself many seasons ago. I didn't have a clue what it was, or how to fix it. But you did, Tinker Bell. You are quite a rare talent."

Tink beamed, feeling embarrassed and pleased at the same time.

"I'd imagine there's someone out there who's missing this," Fairy Mary added.

Tinker Bell looked up. "What do you mean?"

Queen Clarion and Fairy Mary exchanged a sly look.

"I think perhaps a certain tinker fairy has a job to do after all . . . on the mainland!" Fairy Mary said in her usual bossy tone.

Tinker Bell's heart filled with joy. "You mean . . ."

The queen nodded.

Tinker Bell was so happy she wanted to dart into the air and turn somersaults. The mainland! She, Tinker Bell, was going to the mainland to help deliver spring. Her wings trembled with emotion. What an honor!

Her friends cheered, but suddenly Tinker Bell felt a stab of worry. She turned to the queen. "Thank you, Your Highness! But . . . how will I find who it belongs to?"

"You'll know," Queen Clarion assured Tink, just as she had assured her on the day she had arrived. "Now go!" Her voice was kind, but Tinker Bell recognized that she—and everyone else—had just been given a command.

Springtime Square erupted as the fairies snapped into action.

Tinker Bell bowed to the queen and hurried to do as she was ordered.

But then she stopped. There was one last thing she had to do. She threw her arms around Fairy Mary and gave her a huge hug.

"Good heavens!" Fairy Mary exclaimed, half pleased and half shocked.

"Thank you," Tinker Bell said. She turned and started to fly away again, but Terence ran up and stopped her.

"Tink! I have something to help you on the mainland." He put a tiny leaf package in her hand.

"Oh, Terence. That's so sweet."

"Good luck, Tink," he said.

At that moment, Tink's friends swept her into the air. It was time to go. Time to fly. There was not a moment to lose.

Tink watched Clank and Bobble struggle to lift the music box.

Queen Clarion knew just what to do. She flew by and playfully sprinkled Bobble, Clank, and the music box with some extra pixie dust.

VOOOM!

Up into the air they flew, carrying the music box—and thrilled to be joining the nature fairies and Tinker Bell on this great adventure. They knew that *this* was going to be a special spring indeed.

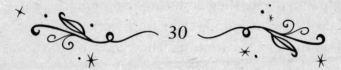

On the mainland, in the city of London, Kensington Gardens wore the last days of winter like a shabby old coat.

But it wouldn't have to endure the cold much longer. Up in the sky, a magical procession was approaching.

Light fairies, animal fairies, garden fairies, water fairies, flower fairies, painting fairies, planting fairies, and—for the first time ever—tinker fairies flew overhead in sparkling clouds and singing clusters.

The Minister of Spring pointed over the London rooftops. "Fairies to the north! Fairies to the south! To the east and west!"

Fairies fanned out in every direction, doing what they did best.

Tinker Bell swiftly followed a group down into Kensington Gardens and watched as her fellow fairies performed tiny miracles. A light fairy directed the sun's rays and melted away the last bit of frost that was still clinging to a frozen branch.

A water fairy used pixie dust to clean up the cloudy water of a pond.

Animal fairies gently woke sleeping squirrels.

Tinker Bell flew up high so that she could watch. The garden fairies hurried well-behaved rows of marching flower bulbs into their beds. The bulbs planted themselves and waited while the water fairies sprinkled them with rain.

Trees bloomed.

Baby birds took to the air.

Rainbows shot across the sky in every direction.

The grubby gray winter coat was gone now, replaced with the gorgeous garments of spring. Kensington Gardens seemed to explode with life and color like a kaleidoscope.

Tink was mesmerized by all she saw. It was more beautiful than she had ever imagined.

Just then, she heard a whistle and saw Clank and Bobble waving at her, reminding her that she had a job to do.

She tried to take the music box from them, but it was too heavy to carry by herself. Tink remembered that she had Terence's gift in her pocket.

She opened the little package and smiled. Extra pixie dust!

Tinker Bell sprinkled some dust on the music box

and held the box by the dancer's hand.

By twilight, Tinker Bell was exhausted. She hadn't found the owner of the music box.

Queen Clarion had said Tink would know whose it was. But how?

Suddenly, as Tink flew past a window, the music box began to glow.

She fluttered back and hovered just outside the window. The music box glowed even more brightly. This had to be it.

Tinker Bell gently set the music box down on the windowsill and peered through the glass. "Wow!" she whispered. There were toys and lovely, shiny things everywhere.

A door inside the house opened. Someone was coming. Quick as lightning, Tinker Bell placed the music box on the windowsill. Then she tapped on the glass and ducked behind a nearby chimney, where she could watch without being seen.

A little girl ran to the window and opened it. When she saw the music box, her eyes lit up.

She lifted the box happily, as if it were a long-lost friend. Then the little girl pulled out a small key on a chain around her neck. She put the key into the music box and turned it.

Tink moved closer to the window, eager to see what the little girl was doing.

Wonder of wonders, once the key was turned, the music box began to play all on its own.

The little girl cradled the box in her arms and listened as if it were the most beautiful sound in the world.

Tinker Bell watched with satisfaction and giggled.

The little girl heard the laugh and looked up.

Tinker Bell quickly darted back out of sight, her heart pounding. Eventually, the little girl turned away.

"Mummy!" she cried. "Guess what? Guess what?"

"Yes, Wendy, what is it?" a voice answered.

Tinker Bell smiled at a job well done. She opened her wings and took to the air, soaring into the golden sunset where Iridessa, Fawn, Silvermist, and Rosetta were waiting.

Their work here was done.

It was time to go home.

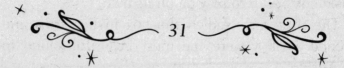

Queen Clarion stood on the balcony of her royal apartment, her eyes glued to the beautiful sky over Pixie Hollow. Once again, her thoughts were of the mainland.

She could picture the way Kensington Gardens looked in its new spring colors. The way the fairies were gathering in the sky from every corner of London, preparing to return to Pixie Hollow.

The queen heard the jingling laughter as the fairies flew past Big Ben, along the Thames River, and over Tower Bridge.

Queen Clarion had waited all night, not sleeping a wink—and she wouldn't rest until every fairy had safely returned. Her butterfly friend had come to keep her company again and sat on her shoulder.

She spoke playfully to him to keep herself from worrying. "A fairy's work is much more than at first it might appear. Suppose your broken clock ticks, though it hasn't in a year."

Over the sea the fairies flew. Some touched down briefly on the water, and their jingling laughter echoed across the waves.

Queen Clarion clasped her hands together. So many obstacles. So many dangers.

Finally, the fairies who were playing in the surf were taken up by the wind and carried through the clouds.

Queen Clarion let out her breath and smiled. The fairies were blowing toward the shining Second Star to the Right!

All would be well now.

They were almost home.

The butterfly flew from Queen Clarion's shoulder and fluttered in happy circles, as if he, too, had heard something special.

The queen whispered now, not wanting her voice to drown out the faint sound of laughter. "Perchance you find a toy you lost, or jingling bells you hear. It all means that one very special fairy might be near!"

Up in the distant sky, Queen Clarion saw something appear over the horizon and twinkle. Then she heard a laugh.

The laugh was so infectious, and the twinkle so bright, it could only be one fairy.

Queen Clarion smiled. Here came Tinker Bell, the first fairy over the horizon, leading all the others back to Pixie Hollow.

Where will she lead them next? Queen Clarion wondered, with a laugh of her own. She didn't know. But she was certain that with Tinker Bell around, Pixie Hollow would never be the same.